Puffin Books

The Way to Sattin Shore

Kate Tranter is fatherless – or is she? The evidence of the tombstone she finds in the churchyard seems conclusive. And yet . . .

The tombstone disappears: and Kate is left with a mystery about which her family either knows nothing or will tell nothing. Her search for the truth leads to Sattin Shore: and the way to Sattin Shore turns out to be a way into the past. One dark night, years before, a man – who was he? – had drowned on Sattin Shore. And that same day, by more than mere coincidence, a baby had been born. Kate herself.

But Kate lives in the present, as well as with the riddles of the past. She is close companion to the family cat, the gloriously golden Syrup, whose adventures criss-cross her own. She makes a new friend at school, with whom to share what secrets can be shared. She has two older brothers: one introduces her to the snowy delights of tobogganing: the other takes her on a long bike ride in the direction – once again – of Sattin Shore. Then the jigsaw pieces of present and past begin to fit together in Kate's mind: and the finished picture shows a new future, too.

This superb tale is for all who enjoy a mystery lightened by humour and by an awareness of the ups and downs of family life. The reader will be totally engrossed in this beautifully written and compelling story, in which all the characters come alive from the very first page.

Philippa Pearce, the daughter of a flour miller and corn merchant, was the youngest of four children. She was educated at the Perse Girls' School in Cambridge and then at Girton College. She was a scriptwriter and producer for the BBC Schools department, and then worked as an editor for Oxford University Press and André Deutsch. She lives near the mill house where she grew up on the upper reaches of the River Cam.

Other books by Philippa Pearce

THE BATTLE OF BUBBLE AND SQUEAK
A DOG SO SMALL
THE ELM STREET LOT
MRS COCKLE'S CAT
MINNOW OF THE SAY
LION AT SCHOOL AND OTHER STORIES
THE SHADOW-CAGE AND OTHER TALES OF THE SUPERNATURAL
TOM'S MIDNIGHT GARDEN
WHAT THE NEIGHBOURS DID
WHO'S AFRAID AND OTHER STRANGE STORIES

Philippa Pearce

The Way to Sattin Shore

Illustrated by Charlotte Voake

Puffin Books

PUFFIN BOOKS

Published by the Penguin Group
27 Wrights Lane, London w8 5tz, England
Viking Penguin Inc., 40 West 23rd Street, New York, New York 10010 USA
Penguin Books Australia Ltd, Ringwood, Victoria, Australia
Penguin Books Canada Ltd, 2801 John Street, Markham, Ontario, Canada l3r 1b4
Penguin Books (NZ) Ltd, 182–190 Wairau Road, Auckland 10, New Zealand

Penguin Books Ltd, Registered Offices: Harmondsworth, Middlesex, England

First published by Kestrel Books 1983
Published in Puffin Books 1985
Reprinted 1985, 1986, 1987, 1988

Made and printed in Great Britain
by Richard Clay Ltd, Bungay, Suffolk
Set in Photina

Library of Congress Catalog card number: 84–23729
(CIP data available)

CONTENTS

1.	The Beam of Darkness	7
2.	Saturday Morning	15
3.	The Jigsaw Puzzle	24
4.	Snow	30
5.	Gone!	43
6.	Other People; other places	51
7.	Nor Cat Nor Rat	59
8.	Out of School	67
9.	Mrs Randall Climbs the Stairs	79
10.	Eyes in the Mirror	89
11.	Kate with Anna	99
12.	Syrup	107
13.	Thirst at Midnight	112
14.	Nan	118
15.	Kate Goes Back	127
16.	The Tale of a Dead Man	134
17.	Two Pillows	142
18.	Strawberry-picking	151
19.	A Statue on the Stairs	160
20.	Homecoming	165
21.	In the Café	173
22.	Along Sattin Shore	181

Chapter 1

THE BEAM OF DARKNESS

Here is Kate Tranter coming home from school in the
January dusk – the first to come, because she is the
youngest of her family. Past the churchyard. Past
the shops. Along the fronts of the tall, narrow terrace
houses she goes. Not this one, nor this one, nor this ...

Stop at the house with no lit window.

This is home.

Up three steps to the front door, and feel for the key
on the string in her pocket. Unlock, and then in. Stand
just inside the door with the door now closed, at her back.

Stand so, in the hall. Ahead, to the right, the stairs.
Ahead, to the left, the passage to the kitchen: in the wider
part, by the back door, a round, red, friendly eye has seen
her – the reflector of her bicycle.

To the left of the hall, Granny's room.

Kate Tranter took a slow breath. She made herself ready
to start across the floor to the stairs – to cross the dark
beam that came from her grandmother's room through
the gap where her grandmother's door stood ajar.

On a weekday, at this time, her grandmother's eyes
were always turned to that door, as she sat in her room

by the window. Her eyes looked out through the crack of the door, on the watch for whoever came in, whoever went out. Whoever came in must cross her line of vision to go down the passage to the kitchen, or to go upstairs. Whoever went out was seen, noted.

Sometimes, it was true, Granny might sit with her eyes closed. Sometimes, perhaps, she dozed.

But, as long as the door stood ajar, Granny was there, the watcher. When she went to bed, or when she went out walking, the door was shut. Only then.

Now she did not call out: 'Is that you, Kate?' or even 'Hello!' But then, she never called out.

Kate took her breath and started off across the beam of darkness to the stairs. She reached the stairs and went up them – up, past her mother's room and Randall's room, that used to be hers; and then up again to her own attic bedroom, opposite Lenny's.

Her door, too, stood well ajar; but that was a good sign. She knew what – *whom* – to expect.

She pushed the door wide: 'Syrup?' And put on the light for a moment, for the pleasure of seeing the glow spring up in Syrup's golden fur as he lounged on the bed. He did not open his eyes or make a sound, but he stretched his body a little, twisted it a little, until he lay with his soft, pale underbelly fur upwards, and his front legs extended over his head, his eyes still closed, the end of his tongue caught between his teeth. His tail with its bent end – his only imperfection – lay still.

Kate turned the light off again, and waited for her eyes to accustom themselves to the dimness. Then she sat down on the bed beside him and tickled him in the armpits; and he curled his front paws and then uncurled them again . . .

Hard to know how much he liked being tickled; but, at least, he did not get up and go away from her.

She lay down on the bed beside him, to caress him at ease. She tickled him, stroked him, chirruped to him and purred to him. He began to purr back.

'Oh, Syrup!' she whispered. 'My beautiful, beautiful Syrupy-puss!'

Far down below the front door bell rang. One of the boys could have forgotten his key; not Mum, though. Lenny or Ran – Ran so early? – would go on ringing and ringing.

After a pause, sure enough, another ring.

She and Syrup lay still, waiting.

Suppose Granny went to the door and opened it? – But she never would.

A voice called – it must be through the letterbox: 'Cath!'

A girl's voice; and only at school was she ever called Cath or Catharine. This was probably Anna, from two streets away.

Again, 'Cath!'

Yes, Anna.

It was a long way to go down to open the front door; but, on the other hand, she liked Anna, in a way. She would have to leave Syrup to go down; and then – what would Anna want? She was a friendly soul. She had a petted cat at home, and she knew the Tranters had one. She had said she would like to see Syrup. That was nice . . .

So perhaps Kate *would* go down and open the front door to Anna. Together they could mount the stairs again to Syrup.

But first they must cross the beam of darkness . . .

'Catheeeee!'

No.

She and Syrup lay motionless. The voice did not come again. Kate could imagine the flap of the letterbox falling, the footsteps going away, disappointed. Any caller would think, an empty house – a dead house.

She turned back to Syrup, fondling, whispering.

The room darkened; the whole house darkened. It was very still and quiet, too, with only old Mrs Randall on the ground floor and Kate Tranter in her attic bedroom. And Syrup.

But, through the deepening dusk, footsteps were coming to the house, converging on it from different directions, coming home.

The next arrivals were Lenny and a friend. Kate heard them coming in through the front door, with Lenny's key, then scuffling and whispering and snickering their way upstairs to Lenny's room. They went in and shut the door behind them.

Syrup purred on, and Kate tickled and stroked.

The front door opened again, and there was a bustling through to the kitchen. Syrup stopped purring and lay quite still: was he listening, or perhaps smelling the air? Before Kate had noticed anything, he had scented the fish that Mrs Tranter was about to fry in the kitchen downstairs. Quickly, neatly, he dropped from the bed to the floor, and then out through the still-open door of the bedroom.

'Syrup!' Kate pleaded; but he had gone. She lay on her bed, abandoned. Now she realized how cold she had become, lying there for so long in an unheated attic. Cold and lonely.

She would go downstairs too.

She went out on to the little attic landing. A light shone from under Lenny's door, but there was no sound. The two of them would be working on something, reading instructions, applying rules, constructing, repairing.

She descended to the next landing, and to Randall's room, dark. He was seldom home early nowadays. His room would be empty.

She listened, checking that she could hear no feet

moving in Lenny's room above, no feet downstairs in the hall. Then she opened Ran's door – quickly, quietly – and slipped inside, closing it behind her.

She knew the room, anyway, because once it had been her room. She had been the baby, who had to sleep within earshot of her mother; and the boys had slept in the two attics above. Then she had grown older, and the boys had begun to quarrel, and their mother had rearranged the bedrooms.

What had been her bedroom was now Ran's; what had been his, in the attic, was now hers: she liked that. But she had liked Ran's bedroom most when it had been in the attic. She had often gone there, in those days, and he had never minded. He had let his little sister play with his things and scatter them about. Kate used to stare at Ran's posters and listen to his records and finger his collections; and he had talked to her and teased her and sometimes even played with her and told her stories.

Not any more. Ran was not like that now, and his room had changed, too, much more than just by his moving down from the attic. The record player and records were gone, she was not sure where. The posters had been taken down over the years and not replaced. His collections had all gone. Ran was less and less in his room, and his room told less and less about him. It had grown secretive.

By the light from the street lamp outside, she could see all that was to be seen in the room. There was Ran's bed, made neatly every morning before he left the house – so different from Lenny's or hers. There was his chest-of-drawers, bare-topped. A cupboard for his clothes, the doors shut. A shelf of books, all to do with his evening classes; they told her nothing she wanted to know. A table to work at, and a reading lamp, and a chair.

Kate searched the room with her eyes; but that was all.

She closed her eyes, and concentrated with her other senses. She could hear the ticking of Ran's alarm clock from beside his bed ... Faintly she could smell brilliantine – the faintest of smells that Ran still left behind him when he was at greatest pains to be unnoticed, absent ...

From below her mother called up the stairs: 'Come on! Tea's ready!' Instantly Kate slipped from the room and began going downstairs. She heard Lenny and his friend on the move behind her.

Mrs Tranter, pleasantly flushed by her cooking, was just dishing up. Syrup had crouched on a chair to watch her. The table was half laid, and Kate finished it – with an extra place for Lenny's friend, Brian – and sat down. The two boys came clattering in and sat down, too. Mrs Tranter smiled at Brian. He dropped in quite often, and she liked that for Lenny. She began serving the fish and pouring the tea.

She had already prepared a little tray with a cup of tea and some bread and butter. 'Will you take it, Kate?'

Kate took the tray from the kitchen towards her grand-mother's room. In the hall she paused, hearing footsteps coming up to the front door. Someone fumbled with the letterbox. Only the postman, then – but did the postman ever come as late as this?

A letter flipped through the door and on to the matting, face upwards. She could read the name, in brightest violet ink: MRS RANDALL. The envelope bore no stamp, no postmark: it had been delivered by hand, but not by the postman's hand.

The footsteps went briskly away; and then a car – whose engine had been left running – drove off.

Kate did not stand wondering. She picked up the letter and added it to what was already on the tray, and passed on.

Even before she pushed her grandmother's door fully open, she reached in to switch on the light. Then she entered. With light, the room seemed ordinary. So seemed Granny, too, blinking at the electric glare, and clearing things from the little table beside her, to make space for the teatray. She was murmuring, 'Tea already!' and 'You're a good girl, Kate ...'

As Kate edged the tray on to the table, Mrs Randall saw her letter. She picked it up, stared at it. Then she hooked a knobbled finger under the flap of the envelope and began slowly, clumsily to tear it open.

Kate drew the curtains close and was going back to the kitchen.

'Leave the door ajar,' said her grandmother; and the sound of tearing paper slowly went on.

Kate was back in the kitchen, just sitting down again to her fish, when there was a cry from her grandmother's room – her grandmother's voice raised almost to a shout: 'Catharine! Catharine!'

Mrs Tranter started up and ran. From the kitchen they heard her exclaim: 'Whatever is it, Mother?' And old Mrs Randall's: 'Look at this! Look – look!'

Then the door was shut, and the voices behind it sank and were muffled.

Lenny was still concentrating on his fish, but Brian asked: 'What's upset your gran, then?'

Lenny said: 'Oh, something, I suppose ...'

Brian said: 'She's not usually like that, is she?'

Lenny had his mouth full, so Kate said, 'No. But per-haps ...' She thought of the letter on the tray, but did not speak of it.

'Perhaps what?'

'Nothing.'

They went on with their tea. After a while, Mrs Tranter came back. She sat down in front of the teapot, and began slowly to pour herself a cup of tea. She seemed deep in thought, remote from them all.

'What was the matter?' asked Brian.

Recalled, Mrs Tranter was startled and confused. 'What was what matter?'

'With their gran, when she shouted out?'

Like Kate, Mrs Tranter answered: 'Nothing ... nothing ...' She was looking at Brian without really seeing him; then, more attentively: 'You're an inquisitive boy, aren't you?'

'I like to know things,' said Brian, 'so I have to find things out. I ask.'

Kate felt respect, and also envy.

Later that evening, as usual, old Mrs Randall went to the bathroom, while her daughter tidied her room, preparing it for the night. When she had done that and gone back to the kitchen, Mrs Randall was still in the bathroom.

Kate tiptoed into her grandmother's room. The bedside light was now on. Everything was neat and tidy. No pieces of paper lying about. She looked into the waste-paper basket: nothing – not even an empty envelope.

Her mother had tidied everything away, beautifully.

Chapter 2

SATURDAY MORNING

The next day was Saturday.

Randall had come home on Friday evening only as Kate was going to bed; and this morning he was lying in. Mrs Tranter went out to do the weekend shopping. Lenny went out to meet friends somewhere. Only Kate remained, and Randall in bed – and Granny in her room downstairs.

Kate waited and waited. At last she knocked on Ran's door. There was no answer, so she pushed the door open and looked round it towards the bed. 'Are you awake yet, Ran?' she whispered.

'What?'

'Are you awake?'

'Yes. Now.'

He rolled over so that he was looking at her. The bedding drawn up round his shoulders and head made a dark cave: she could not see his face properly, only his eyes looking at her. 'Well?' he said.

She was nervous. She had not really thought that Ran would be much impressed by the story of the hand-delivered letter and their grandmother's cry, but at least the whole thing made an excuse for talking to him. The excuse now seemed a poor one. All the same, she told him the story.

'Well?' he said, at the end.

'Well, don't you think it was funny – I mean, odd – what happened?'

'I don't think it was odd or not odd. It's just none of our business.'

'But it's our grandmother, and it happened in our house!'

'Not our house; her house.'

'Well, in our home.'

'Oh, go away, Kate! You talk a lot of rubbish!'

She felt like crying. She didn't really mind what he had just said, only that *he* had said it. Suddenly she thought she might as well cry, after all: she burst into tears. The eyes from the bed watched her. Not long ago Ran would have said: 'Come on, Kate, you'll be soaked with salt water! Come on, Katy, there's a good girl!' Now he said: 'You decided to cry, didn't you?'

'You don't care!' she shouted. 'Nobody cares!'

'What is there to care about?'

'I hate you!'

She rushed from his room, slamming the door behind her, and ran downstairs, burning with the resolution to run out of her brother's life for ever and ever.

She picked up her jacket. Her bicycle would be waiting for her by the back door. She flew towards it.

Kate was the only one allowed to keep her bicycle in the passage by the back door: the other two were supposed always to put theirs away in the shed at the bottom of the garden. But here was Ran's bicycle left in the passage-way since last night, and left right on top of hers!

She fell upon the bicycles, to wrest them apart and take her own; but the passageway was narrow and the bicycles, though taken momentarily by surprise, rallied as one machine in self-defence. Ran's right pedal en-meshed itself among the spokes of Kate's back wheel, so that when she hauled Ran's bicycle up, her own came with it. With furious strength she raised both bicycles and tried to shake them apart. The weight was too much, her grip failed, and the machines fell, still locked together, on her foot.

She cried aloud, more in rage than pain. She did not hear the front door opening as her mother came in with the Saturday shopping. Mrs Tranter rested baskets and bags on the floor while she put away the front door key; and she watched Kate and the bicycles.

Now Kate had begun, with the wildest savagery, to shake, bang, push, pull; in return, the bicycles clattered and ground together, pedals whirred, drop handlebars swung viciously against soft flesh, the curved end of a brake handle snatched at Kate's jersey neck in passing, and the innocent-seeming three-inch projection of cal-lipered brake-cable on the back wheel of Kate's bicycle turned out not to be innocent at all, but a weapon for trying to gouge an eye out –

'Kate!' said her mother just loudly enough, and Kate heard her and paused, breathless. Mrs Tranter came forward and took hold of the uppermost bicycle and held it steady, for Kate to disentangle the one underneath: 'Now, Kate!'

When the two bicycles were free of each other, Mrs Tranter wheeled Ran's machine a few feet forward, so that Kate could move hers right out of its range, towards the back door. Then Mrs Tranter leaned her son's bicycle back again where it should not have been in the first place. She said: 'Ran is in the wrong; but you were very silly, Kate.'

That was all. Mrs Tranter's way had never been to ques-tion, wonder, discuss. Kate was left to the privacy of her feelings.

Kate opened the back door and wheeled her bicycle into the garden. Thence she could take it into the side alley and away.

She was distracted from her original purpose by the sight of Syrup crouching on the garden wall, not looking at her, but knowing she was there. She coaxed him to come to her, but he never moved: he knew he was out of her reach as long as she held on to her bicycle.

Then, while she still cajoled, he rose to his paws, yawned, stretched, and began to pace along the top of the wall. She called to him to stop, but he paid no attention.

He went from the wall of the Tranters' back garden to the wall of their neighbours', and on. Syrup was well known at certain houses in the neighbourhood. In the same street, there was a house where he drank milk and was referred to as Ginger. Further away – and quite unknown to Kate as yet – he ate fish and chicken scraps and went by the name of Sunshine, or Sunny Jim.

This morning he was on one of his longer expeditions.

'You!' Kate called after him, angrily. Then she gave her attention to the bicycle, pushing it into the alley and so into the street, where she mounted.

But where, after all, should she go?

She resolved to call on Anna. She cycled through the streets to where Anna's block of flats loomed up. She cycled past the block. She stopped, turned her bicycle, and cycled past the block again, so slowly this time that she nearly fell off. She willed Anna to open a window and lean out to shout: 'Wait a minute, Cathy! Don't go! I want to talk to you about something!'

But Anna didn't.

In the end, Kate got off her bicycle, leaned it against some railings, and conscientiously padlocked her front wheel to them. She made her preparations slowly, still giving Anna her chance. But Anna did not take it.

She thought she remembered the flat-number that Anna had once told her. She entered the block, went up to the right floor, found the number, rang the bell.

From inside came the sound of a Hoover at work, and it did not stop. She wondered whether she should ring again. If Anna had been longing for her to call, she surely would have bounced hopefully to the door at once. But she might still be in bed, like Ran.

She rang again, against her better judgement: this was perhaps the wrong flat, after all. The Hoovering went on. Almost certainly the wrong flat.

Suddenly the door was opened by a man in his shirt sleeves and wearing a woman's pinafore. He was dragging a carpet-cleaner behind him, still roaring. He looked cross. With one foot he was fumbling to turn the Hoover off, while he stared at Kate.

Somehow she could not believe this was Anna's father. 'I'm sorry,' Kate said hurriedly. 'I've made a mistake.'

The roar of the Hoover died. 'What?'

'I thought Anna Johnson lived here.'

'Anna? She's gone out to see a friend. Back at dinner-time, I suppose. D'you want to leave a message?'

A kettle began to whine in the background. The man twitched irritably towards the sound. 'A message?'

'Not really. No.' Swiftly the kettle was reaching full whistle. 'Just say, "Cath called."'

'"Catcalled"?'

Was he making fun of her? But he looked crosser than ever. She backed away. 'Don't bother. It's nothing.'

'*Who?*' he cried, exasperated.

The kettle shrieked.

'Nothing!' she shouted. 'Doesn't matter! No!'

She turned her back on him and ran for the stairs. She

heard the door slam behind her. The second door to be slammed that morning.

This was a bad Saturday – one of the worst.

To soothe herself, she rode on to the churchyard, and leaned her bicycle against its wall. She went in among the tombstones. No one knew she sometimes did this. No one knew that she knew exactly where to find her father's grave. She had found it by accident over a year ago. She had been following Syrup along garden walls to the churchyard wall, and she had gone in for the first time then. She had read some of the epitaphs, with their names and dates, on the headstones; and she had at once noticed this one because the date on it was *her* date, exactly.

Here it was, between a white stone cross on one side, and a plinth, with a kind of toddler-angel on top, on the other. A plain tombstone, with a plain inscription. First of all: IN MEMORY OF JAMES TRANTER, and a date half a century earlier. That would be her grandfather, her father's father. Then, below: AND OF HIS SON ALFRED ROBERT TRANTER, and then the date of her own birthday. The date of her birth: the very day and month and year. On an impulse, Kate leant forward and traced with her finger the lettering of the name and the date – her date.

She had been born the day her father had died. She had once been told that, and that this was no mere coincidence. The news of his death – by drowning, wasn't it? – had brought Mrs Tranter early to childbirth. Kate had been born prematurely: a skinny, delicate little thing that the hospital had thought could not live. But she had lived. Here she was.

Someone came round the corner of the church, and Kate jumped. But it was only the vicar.

'Hello there!' he said, and she saw at once that he would

have liked to ask what she was doing in that corner of the churchyard on such a wintry morning; but he didn't want to sound unfriendly.

'I was just looking,' she said, as if she were in a shop crowded with attractive objects for sale.

'Ah!' he said with deep understanding, and passed on.

He was followed almost at once by someone she did know well: Syrup. He came along the top of the churchyard wall, homeward-bound now. This time Kate did not try to detain him, but hurried back to her bicycle to see if she could race him home. Unlikely – he would almost certainly be there first. From her attic window – the only one that overlooked the church and churchyard – she had often observed his expeditions in this direction. (His distinctive tail made him recognizable, even at great distances.) She could never be certain of his destination beyond the churchyard, but certainly for the stretch churchyard-to-home he had worked out the shortest possible route – the safest, too, from dogs, cars, and importunate human beings.

She stood on her pedals most of the way home. She whizzed past a black figure stumping along with a walking-stick: her grandmother, well wrapped up against the cold, on her way back from a morning walk. Old Mrs Randall never saw her, and Kate did not hail her in passing.

At home, she found Syrup already in the kitchen. He was winding himself round the legs of Mrs Tranter as she sat cutting up stewing beef.

'Where's Ran?' Kate asked, not hopefully.

'Gone out. Won't be back. Oh, Kate – someone came for you this morning, but you were out. You know – that girl from your school – Anna.'

'Oh,' said Kate. While she had been to call on Anna, Anna had been calling on her. What had Anna's dad said? – 'Gone to see a friend.' She – Kate – was the friend that Anna had gone to see.

'I might go round to hers this afternoon,' said Kate.

'I shouldn't do that,' said Mrs Tranter, 'because she said she'd call back here again. You'll only miss each other.'

'All right,' said Kate. She was thinking of Syrup: all that exercise this morning – he might be willing to spend the afternoon on her bed. Should she ask Anna up to see him? She might. She could think about it.

'Why don't you ask this friend to stay to tea?' suggested Mrs Tranter. She had made such suggestions before. 'Lenny will probably be out with Brian again. You'd have the house to yourselves, really. You could have tea watching the telly. Ask her.'

'I might,' said Kate. She really might, this time.

Old Mrs Randall now appeared in the kitchen doorway, still hatted and coated from her walk. 'Catharine,' she said, 'there's snow coming before the weekend's over.'

'Surely not, Mother.' Mrs Tranter cast a glance through the kitchen window at the pale blue winter sky.

'Yes. And I want to go to church tomorrow morning, if it's not already snowing. I want you to come with me.'

'Of course, Mother.'

Mrs Randall retreated.

'Snow?' said Kate.

'Your grandmother is usually right,' said Mrs Tranter.

Syrup had begun to mew piteously. Mrs Tranter did not notice him for some time; then she tutted at him and gave him some pieces of fat and gristle from the meat.

'Would there be anything nice for tea?' asked Kate.

'The usual,' said Mrs Tranter. She was impatient because Kate interrupted her thoughts. Kate saw that, and saw that her mother's thoughts were dark. Her mother had already forgotten that Kate's friend might be staying to tea. Well, she wouldn't be staying unless Kate asked her; and suddenly Kate resolved not to.

Kate left the kitchen, without her mother's noticing her going, and went upstairs to the privacy of her attic bedroom.

After all, she could always do some homework.

Chapter 3

THE JIGSAW PUZZLE

The snow came on Sunday afternoon.

In the morning the sky was a greyish-white, thick and even. The air was still and very cold. In such wintry weather old Mrs Randall did not usually venture forth; but she had said she wanted to go to morning service, and she was clearly determined upon it. She went, with one hand clutching her daughter's arm, the other her walking-stick.

Mrs Tranter left instructions for the preparation of Sunday dinner. Lenny was in charge: he would put the vegetables on at the right time, and start the joint in the oven, and regulate the oven-settings. He rather enjoyed all that. Ran need do nothing, because he would be working at his books. Kate had to lay the table, but that could be done in the last ten minutes.

So Kate had the morning to herself. She could be downstairs in the warm living room, or upstairs in her bedroom. Syrup chose the living room, but she preferred her bedroom. She put on two long jerseys and her winter dressing-gown and sat by the window to do one of her Christmas jigsaw puzzles. Every so often she lifted her head to look intently out of the window: she wanted to see the very first snowflake fall.

The jigsaw should not have been a difficult one, but it took a long time. She began to suspect that one or more pieces were missing. She found she was right: one piece was certainly missing, and – because it was missing – she had crammed another awkwardly into its place. So there was one piece misplaced, and also an empty place, a hole in the picture. Even when she had taken out the misplaced piece and fitted it where it should go, there was still the hole. You could say it was not an important hole, because it came in the midst of a crowd of blurred faces in a street scene at Christmas. Everywhere were multicoloured street lights and decorations; all the people were carrying gaily wrapped parcels or even little Christmas trees; but amongst them all was someone without a face. That worried Kate.

Abruptly she remembered to look out of the window, and caught sight of what was perhaps the first snowflake. It came drifting leisurely down, borne slightly now this way, now that, by what must be the minutest of air-ripples. It reached the pavement, touched it gently, and splattered gently, white. It did not melt. The snow was going to lie.

She looked further outward, and still saw only single snowflakes falling here and there. Now she was looking towards the church and churchyard. She could not see the church porch, from which, about now, the congregation would be coming out; but pretty soon she was sure they were out – there were two of them, walking in the churchyard.

She watched two distant figures, both women, she thought, one of them old and partly supported by the other. She watched two women; and then suddenly realized she was watching her own mother and grandmother. They were moving through the churchyard, making for a corner of it – *her* corner. She could not see, at that distance, which of the graves they stopped at, but she could guess. She was certain. In spite of the cold and the beginning of the snowfall, they stopped there for some minutes.

Perhaps they were talking, perhaps not. Perhaps her mother was crying as she stood by her husband's grave; but that did not seem likely, somehow. Kate had seldom heard her mother speak of her dead husband: occasionally he was 'your father' to the three children; even more rarely to Granny he was mentioned as 'Fred'.

Granny would certainly not be crying. After all, Alfred Robert had been her son-in-law, not her son. Besides, Granny could not possibly cry.

They stood in front of the tombstone. Old Mrs Randall lifted her walking-stick and seemed to point to the stone. After that, they began to walk away. This time their pace was hurried. They had become aware of the increasing snow.

They would be home soon.

Kate jumbled up the pieces of the imperfect jigsaw and put them away in their box. She ought to go downstairs to lay the table. But, for a few moments, she could watch the snow falling. Falling? It was driving down now – thicker, faster, until, as though she had seen all that she was to be allowed to see, a dazzling, whirling white curtain was lowered between her and the churchyard.

The whirl and dazzle excited Kate. She felt restless, eager, ready to laugh – or, perhaps, to cry. She went downstairs to the kitchen. She found Lenny there, as she expected, and Ran, too. They stood at the window, side by side, watching the snow. Ran seemed mesmerized by it: he watched attentively, never spoke. Lenny, on the other hand, was excited, as Kate herself was: he fidgeted on his feet, peered, exclaimed, and finally, as Ran paid no attention to his remarks, dug him in the ribs with a wooden cooking spoon that he was still holding.

'Don't!' said Ran.

Kate heard the front door opening: the two churchgoers were returning. They would dispose of their snowy clothing and then come to the kitchen. Kate busied herself with the laying out of knives and forks and spoons and plates on the table. She was no longer watching Lenny and Ran, and so missed the exact sequence of happenings. But she became aware that Lenny had seized the largest saucepan lid as a shield and, brandishing his spoon as a sword, was mimicking an attack on Ran. And Ran was laughing – but angrily – and fending him off.

And then, in an instant, saucepan lid and spoon flew to the ground and the two boys were grappling in real fight, as they had not done since they were much younger. They fought each other to the floor, and there they jarred against the table, sending cutlery sliding and clattering, and they rolled against Kate's legs, and she screamed quite loudly, for the top plate on the pile she was carrying danced at the shock.

From the hall, 'What is it?' cried Mrs Tranter in terror, and burst into the kitchen. She stood on the threshold, snow still lying on her shoulders and head. Their grandmother approached more slowly, from behind.

Lenny and Ran stopped fighting, but their mother had seen them. 'Why do you two have to quarrel?' she demanded. She spoke with the ordinary, commonplace little despair of fed-upness; her question did not expect an answer.

But, from behind her, came old Mrs Randall's voice, as if she were talking only to herself, yet distinctly: 'Quarrelling – fighting: they inherit it . . .'

Kate saw her mother's face change, whiten. She was

staring at the two boys as if she saw them quite differently; or perhaps she saw quite different boys.

'Oh, yes!' the quiet old voice repeated, 'they inherit bad blood, they do . . .'

What did she mean?

Mrs Tranter stood speechless, motionless in the door-way.

Ran said: 'I'm going out to see a friend. I shan't be here for dinner, after all.' He could not very well push past his mother. He touched her on the shoulder, she moved aside, and he was out – past his grandmother – into the hall – and then out through the front door. The front door closed behind him.

Mrs Tranter blinked several times, as if to clear her vision.

Lenny said: 'It was all nothing, really, Mum. Just fooling about. Because of the snow.' He added, 'Sorry!' in a general kind of way, and began to set the cutlery back in position on the table.

Mrs Tranter recovered herself: 'Now for Sunday dinner!' Then, differently: 'But he went out in all that snow just as he was!'

'No, Mum. Honestly!' said Lenny. 'He took his anorak as he went. I saw him. Honestly.'

'Let's get on.'

On this occasion, Sunday dinner was without Ran; but old Mrs Randall ate with the others, as was her custom at weekends. Nobody talked; and the snow still fell outside the window, shutting them into a whitish gloom.

All that afternoon, snow fell, sometimes almost as in a blizzard. It was lying, too. After dinner and the washing up, Lenny gave all his attention to the snow. His mother had forbidden him to go out into it yet; so he moved from window to window of the house, sampling different snow scenes. He talked softly to himself about the snow all the time.

He only grumbled that the snow had come at the end of the weekend. Tomorrow was Monday, school day.

But if the snow would last until next weekend ...

'What then?' asked Kate.

Lenny did not answer, but he smiled and narrowed his eyes, seeing from between narrowed lids visions of snowy delight, pure Paradises of snow. Watching his face, Kate knew what he saw, although she could not see it for herself.

Chapter 4

SNOW

On Monday morning Kate knew by the glare on her bed-room ceiling that there must be snow outside. She drew her curtains back, and stood in wonder. Snow was no longer falling, but it lay deeply. Whiteness covered every-thing. Every level or sloping surface had snow upon it; only the verticals were snow-free and dark, and, even then, snow had drifted and banked itself up on windward sides. Upstanding objects had the appearance of having settled down into the snow; and mere humps and hollows had disappeared altogether under the cover of snow. And the sky, as before, promised still more snow.

If this went on, Kate thought, everything would dis-appear under the soft whiteness of complete cover-up. Nothing would be recognizable any more. Nothing could be known for what it really was.

She went off to school as usual, but the going was slow. She might have walked where others had beaten a way, but she could not resist the deep untrodden snow at the sides of the pavement. Her booted feet sank through the snow at every step, and had to be lifted up again at every step with a deliberate pull.

People said the snow looked like icing on a cake. She thought of their own Christmas cake before Christmas, iced by their mother, decorated by herself. There had been a tiny Father Christmas holding a present-sack in one hand and the paw of a polar bear cub in the other. While the icing was still soft, she had put the Father Christmas and his bear to one side of the top of the cake, as if they were about to cross it. Now, as she plodded to school, she thought *this* was what it would have been like for them to struggle across the deep white icing of the cake-top.

Not all the children managed to reach school that snowy morning; and, anyway, the heating system had broken down, so that the pupils who came were only sent home again. It seemed strange to be home before midday on a Monday. Lenny also came home, but soon after left again to go round to Brian's. He said they were going to build a sledge in Brian's father's workshop. If only – oh, if only the snow would go on! Lenny raised beseeching eyes to the snow-burdened heavens, imploring mercy.

Kate thought again of the white top of her Christmas cake, and the decoration she had decided against using: an Eskimo child on a sledge. The child could hardly have sledged across the top of a dead flat iced cake. You needed quite a steep slope for sledging, which was more than the Christmas cake – or the town of Ipston – could offer.

All that week, on and off, it snowed; and the snow lay, snow on snow, except where the traffic of wheels or feet beat it down. There it became hard-packed, discoloured, and very slippery. Old Mrs Randall gave up her daily walk; and Mrs Tranter slipped and fell on their own front door-step – only, however, breaking a bottle of frozen milk. Randall went off to work, but on foot: cycling was too dangerous. He still went to his evening classes. Lenny and Kate got to their schools late, and came home early. As for Syrup, he stayed indoors for extraordinarily long periods. Mrs Tranter carried him outside twice a day, but he was not grateful.

Anna called on Kate and suggested they made a snowman in the Tranters' back garden, which they did. Lenny did not join in: he made no snowmen, threw no snowballs, slid on no slides. He was feverishly at work in Brian's father's workshop, with Brian.

On Thursday the wind changed, the sun shone in a faint blue sky, and it seemed as if the great thaw had started. Lenny went to bed almost in tears.

But Friday dawned grey and cold again, and the thaw had been slight. Lenny and Brian finished their toboggan. On Friday night there was a hard, hard frost.

On Saturday morning –

'Perfect – *perfect!*' Lenny whispered. He was scarcely able to believe the luck of it.

Lenny's arrangements were all made. Brian's father had agreed to call for him and to drive Lenny and Brian and the sledge to the nearest good slope outside Ipston: Gripe's Hill, towards the estuary. The boys would take a packed lunch, and Brian's father would call for them again at the end of the afternoon.

Ran was also going out somewhere for the day.

That left Kate.

'Why don't you do something in the snow with Anna?' asked Mrs Tranter.

'Anna's going out somewhere, she said,' said Kate.

Lenny shuffled his feet and said reluctantly: 'I suppose Kate could come with us, but one toboggan's not really enough for three people.'

Mrs Tranter frowned. Kate said quickly: 'I was going to stay indoors with Syrup, anyway. He hates the snow, too.'

'Oh, Syrup!' exclaimed Mrs Tranter, as though she were sick of hearing of him.

Lenny was looking cheerful again; but his mother's expression did not change. Lenny went into the kitchen to get his lunch; his mother stayed in the hall, apparently pondering.

Kate went upstairs.

She felt cold in her bedroom because the air was cold; but she felt cold from the inside outwards, too. Although she knew it must be impossible, her stomach felt cold. She felt too cold to cry. Syrup, of course, was downstairs in the warm.

Her mother called her from below, twice, and she went slowly downstairs again. She would not – she would *never* – consent to share that toboggan.

Her mother stood in the hall, smiling up at her. She held something partly behind her back, and now she brought it forward for Kate to see. It was an old-fashioned oblong tray of heavy metal, painted black. A really large tray – larger and stronger than any of the ones stacked in the kitchen for daily use.

Kate gasped. 'But that's Granny's own tray, from her room!' (Even in her amazement, she spoke in a lowered voice. She glanced at the door, always ajar.) She could hardly believe what must have been done: 'She didn't say I could use it?'

'No,' said her mother, also whispering. 'I didn't even ask.' Mrs Tranter did not say how she had managed to get the large tray out of her mother's room without old Mrs Randall's knowledge; but Kate's mother could be resourceful.

Kate took the tray. It was beautifully heavy – she had never handled it before. The tray had belonged to Mrs Randall's mother, who had been in service. It had been given her from the great kitchens where she worked, when she got married. So it was older than Kate's own grandmother; and it had always stood in the same place in her grandmother's room, propped against the wall. It was never moved, never used.

Kate said: 'But suppose – suppose –' She could not think of the right disaster. Such a tray would never break or buckle; she herself would never, never mislay or lose it. 'Suppose I *chipped* the black paint?'

'Suppose you *chipped* the black paint!' repeated her mother. She took Kate by the shoulders and stooped until they were face to face. She brought her face very close to Kate's: 'So *what*?'

Kate felt a kind of wild joy that was only partly at the prospect of tobogganing on the tray over the snow. She gave a little gasping laugh.

Mrs Tranter drew back, as if she thought she might have gone too far. She said: 'Remember, it's on *my* responsibility.' She added: 'Do you think I didn't slide on that tray when I was a little girl? Your gran let me. That's why I thought of it. Now go and get warm things on, while I get you some lunch. The car will be here any minute.'

Anorak, with packed lunch in pocket – boots – gloves – scarf – bobble hat – and she was ready! Kate dashed out to the car just after Lenny. She carried her wonderful tray.

Brian's father opened the boot of the car to put the tray in, and there was the new sledge. While Brian's father eased the tray underneath it, Kate touched the sledge. Lenny watched her. She stroked the wood of the sledge – the long sides, the cross-pieces, the bit at the front where you held on as you lay along the length of the sledge; she fingered the brand-new piece of cord tied from side to side at the front. 'Lovely!' she said of it all. 'It's lovely, Lenny!' And she knew that he liked her saying that – loved her for it. In its own way, the sledge was as magnificent as the iron tray – and Lenny and Brian had made it. It occurred to Kate – with certainty – that *she* could have made a sledge, if there had been someone to tell her how to do it, and if she had had the wood and the tools and the screws and the workshop to do it all in. She would really have needed a father, with a workshop, as Brian had. Then she could have done it.

Now they were all getting into the car. The two boys sat at the back, and Kate sat beside the driver, Brian's father. He did not talk to her, except to say when he would call back for them all.

The drive took some time, because no one dared go fast along these snowy roads into the country. But at least the snow was beginning to be well beaten down: a good many people had decided to go to Gripe's Hill today.

Brian's father stopped at the bottom of the hill long enough to unload the sledging party, and then was away again.

Lenny and Brian started up the hill, dragging their sledge after them. Kate followed more slowly with her tray, which was large enough to be awkward to carry. She stared wonderingly around her as she climbed. She had been on the hill before, in summer, on a school picnic. She remembered short, dark green turf, and the heat of the sun on the picnickers, and the games they had played; but she could not remember *this*. How could she recognize something so utterly changed from what it had been? Gripe's Hill now was another place – all snow, and new and strange. Sunshine gilded the snow-surfaces in front of her, and, behind her, there followed a misshapen shadow, blue-purple on the snow, that was Kate carrying her tray.

Now, as they trudged up through the snow, other people were careering down to one side of them on toboggans or sledges of every kind. Some were home-made; some were smartly painted or varnished shop-ware. People without toboggans or sledges were using trays or anything else that would slide over compacted snow. One little boy was using the lid of his mother's twin-tub washing machine. Another child shot by on a flattened dustbin lid. Another, on a plastic dustbin bag partly stuffed with snow.

For the first time Kate wondered how she would like the experience of tobogganing – the headlong speed, the unstoppable rush of it.

Then they had reached the top of Gripe's Hill. From here opened a far view of snowbound countryside, with snowy fields and hedges and snowy houses, and the dark thread of the road with an occasional car creeping carefully along it. In the furthest distance – 'Look, there!' – Lenny pointed to what must be the estuary. Kate peered and peered, but sun on snow dazzled her, hiding from her eyes what they strained to see.

And now Lenny and Brian were preparing to try out their sledge. For the first run, they must go down together. They piled on, and pushed off, down and away. Kate watched them with misgiving.

They dragged the sledge up again, exclaiming with excitement; and Kate still stood there with her tray. Lenny suggested that she tried it out. She said she would wait.

So, this time, Lenny went down alone on the sledge, while Brian waited with Kate. Then Lenny dragged it to the top again; and then Brian went down on it alone.

While Brian was bringing the sledge back, Lenny showed Kate how she must use her tray. He put it in just the right position, and made her slither on to it and sit down.

'You steer,' he said, 'by leaning your weight to one side or the other.'

'How do people stop?' asked Kate.

'You brake by sticking a heel out into the snow, or

both heels. Keep well away from that huge snowball that some idiot's made halfway down. Go straight down, past it.'

Kate said quickly: 'But not yet, Lenny.'

Lenny was still too excited by his own sledging to be patient with Kate. He cried, 'Right!' and gave the back of the tray a strong push.

It started down the slope so slowly that Kate had time to exclaim: 'I said, *Not yet!*' and to think she might get off the tray while it was moving. Then it was moving too fast. She had to grip the sides. The tray had gathered speed and was shooting down the main sledge-way – faster – faster –

She was bracing her feet against the front rim of the tray and clutching with her hands at the side rims and feeling herself crouch forward and lean back in one contradictory motion. The air flew by her and powdered snow flickered up against her face. She was going so fast that she had no time to think of danger. She was going so fast she had no time to think of anything.

She could not think –

Air – snow – speed – speed –

She saw people streaming past her as they trudged uphill. She saw Brian, and his mouth was open as he shouted something to her.

She saw a great heap of packed snow lying to one side of the track and looming fast towards her, and her dazed mind still had in it Lenny's 'Keep well away!' – A snowball? This was a mountain!

Lenny had said, 'Lean to one side' – but she was already leaning to one side – she was veering off the track, straight for the mountain –

The mountain! –

Now!

Banged – battered – jolted – and then she had stopped.

Everything had stopped, except that her body still seemed to judder with the shock of impact.

Snow was in her hair and mouth and down her neck. She lay in snow; and pretty soon people began to be there and say: 'Are you all right?'

Someone said: 'My! That was a daring thing to do!'

Someone else said: 'Katy! Katy! Are you all right?' And that was Ran, who wasn't here at all, but somewhere else – surely he'd said so, hadn't he?

And Lenny was there, and Ran said: 'What a stupid thing to let her go and do!'

And Lenny said despairingly: 'But I told her NOT to!'

And all the time Ran was helping her up. 'Come *on*, Katy!' And she put her arms round his neck and he hauled her right up out of the snow where she was buried. He began beating the remaining snow off her. The other people had gone now, except for Ran and Lenny and a girl who seemed to be with Ran and who seemed familiar.

And, extraordinarily, Anna was there too; and she was saying, 'But, Cath, you came tobogganing after all! Why wouldn't you come with me, when I asked you?'

But Ran was the one who insisted: 'Say something, Kate! Are you all right, Kate? Say something!'

Kate said, with difficulty: 'Right.' And she realized that she was, too. Just bruised and breathless and very nearly speechless: that was all.

Ran had got hold of one end of the black tray that had buried itself deep in the monster snowball. He tugged at it, and suddenly the whole tray came out – and a good deal of the snowball with it. The tray was quite unharmed.

Ran said: 'Isn't this Granny's own tray?'

'Yes,' said Kate, nodding her head and glad to find that it could be nodded.

'Did she just hand it over?'

Kate tried shaking her head from side to side, and that worked too. 'Mum,' she explained.

'It's a lovely tray for tobogganing,' said Anna, peering under Ran's arm. 'Could I try with it, Cath?'

'Careful!' said Kate with all the emphasis she could manage.

'Of course! And you can have a go with my slider.' Anna was carrying a kind of very large plastic saucer with a handle to each side.

Now Ran took one of Kate's arms and Vicky – yes, that was her name: Kate remembered her doing a newspaper round with Ran once upon a time – Vicky took the other, and they began helping her back up Gripe's Hill again. Lenny came behind with the tray. Kate did not know why she was going to the top of the hill again, considering that she was never going to toboggan again in all her life, ever.

When they reached the top, things began to happen all over again in a way she could not prevent. Anna went shooting off downhill on the black tray – that was all right; and then Ran had put down Anna's slider for Kate. Oh! if only she need not disappoint Ran: but she made no move towards the slider. So he lifted her gently under the arms and set her on it, and helped her to sit down. She did not want to, but Ran thought she did. He set her hands on the side-grips. She made a last attempt never ever to toboggan again: 'Ran, it's very important – just one thing –'

Ran said: 'It's simple, Katy: you lean this way to go that way, and that way to go this way. You were very brave about that snowball, but don't risk it again. Good luck!' And he pushed her off.

The saucer was not as fast as the tray, and it turned round as it began going down, so that for a moment she was looking back at Ran and Vicky, who were standing with arms entwined; and they smiled at her and waved. Then round the slider went again, and then faster and faster, and this time she did think, and she leaned in the right way and shot safely past the ruined snowball and on towards the bottom of the hill –

'Oooooh!' she whooped, and not just in terror.

– And at the bottom, going so fast, shot right off the slider and was suddenly on top of Anna – or rather, on top of the black tray, which was on top of Anna, as though the black tray had been tobogganing on Anna, instead of the other way about. Anna had just been getting up out of the snow, but now she was back in it again. At last they both managed to get up, gasping, and laughing between the gasps. They fell into each other's arms and hugged each other for joy. Then Anna picked up the plastic saucer, and Kate picked up her black tray, and they staggered back up the hill together, for another go.

From now on they used only the black tray – there was plenty of room for both of them at once, one behind the other, in a tight clasp. They went faster down the hill than Kate ever dreamed they could; and at the bottom they always flew off the tray and landed deep in the snow, and struggled up from it, and gasped and laughed and blamed each other and the snow, and collected the tray again and took it up the hill again.

For another go.

Once Ran asked if he might borrow Granny's tray from Kate, and he and Vicky went down on it together. When they came back, Vicky said: 'Your tray's better than any toboggan. Truly!' She and Ran had the use only of an old sledge borrowed from friends of Vicky.

They ate their packed lunches so late that the sun was beginning to set in a red dazzle across the snow. Anna had to leave the hill, to get her lift home. 'I wish I could stay with you,' she said sorrowfully to Kate; and Kate said, 'I wish so, too.' After Anna had gone, she still sledged on the black tray, but there was nobody to laugh with in the snow at the bottom.

And now Brian's father would be waiting for them. They all went down together, and Randall begged a lift for himself and Vicky. As biggest, he had to sit in the front with Brian's father, and the other four squashed in the back. Two sledges and a tray went into the boot.

When they reached Brian's house, Brian's father made them all come in. They crowded into the kitchen, and Brian's mother gave them mugs of tea and slices of the last of her Christmas cake. They sat round the kitchen table, eating and drinking and talking. But Kate sat in silence. She thought: This is me, drinking tea out of a big yellow mug, and eating Christmas cake, and sitting next to Ran, after tobogganing all day with my friend, Anna.

She felt warm and sleepy, and her muscles felt far too tired ever to let her move again. But now Ran said they must go home, and Vicky said the same. Lenny left the sledge with Brian for the time being, but Kate took her tray, and Vicky took her sledge – only Ran carried it for her.

Kate was so tired that she dropped the black tray twice in the street as they went along. It would have made a great clatter but for the snow it fell on. After the second time, Lenny took charge of it.

At Vicky's house, Kate and Lenny went slowly on, while Ran and Vicky said goodnight at the front gate. Kate said to Lenny: 'That must be where Ran keeps his record player and all his records. I expect they play them often.'

Lenny said, 'What do you mean?'

Kate said, 'Oh, never mind!' And Ran caught them up.

At last they were home, and Kate had crossed the beam of darkness without even noticing it. But Lenny remembered to sidle under cover of the other two, with the tray held out of sight.

Mrs Tranter came out of the kitchen, upset. 'Wherever have you all been, so late? I was really worrying . . .'

They explained; and Ran said, 'You know you fuss, Mum!' and Lenny said, 'We came as quick as we could!' and Kate said, 'It was lovely – lovely!' She sat on the bottom step of the stairs to pull her boots off, and leaned her head against the wall for a moment, and was instantly asleep.

Chapter 5

GONE!

All her life Kate remembered that Saturday on Gripe's Hill. They went tobogganing again on Sunday, and it was good, but not quite so good.

The Sunday afternoon's sport ended in Lenny's spraining his ankle. (Going very fast down the hill, he had braked too suddenly and strongly with one foot.) He was not in great pain, but he could only just hobble. He had to be helped to the car waiting for them at the bottom of the hill. No more tobogganing for Lenny, for the time being.

But that was all right: the season was ending, anyway, with the thaw. At home, Mrs Tranter had made up a temporary bed for Lenny on the couch downstairs, in front of the television set. Here he lay, with his ankle raised, not at all discontented. His satisfaction came less from the unlimited television than from the steady sound of the drip of snow melting from the house roof. He was missing nothing (except school) by being kept indoors, an invalid for a while.

The snows were really over, not to return. The black tray had to be smuggled back into old Mrs Randall's room, to its usual position there. The toboggan that Lenny and Brian had made must be put away until next winter. The toboggan could have stayed with Brian, in his house; but Lenny had already suggested the Tranters' loft, knowing that Brian would like an excuse to work the trapdoor and the loft-ladder. And Brian was eager to do this, even without Lenny's help.

The trapdoor into the loft – the only way into it – was in the ceiling over the top landing, between the door into Kate's room and the door into Lenny's. The trapdoor could be opened only by a loft-pole, which Mrs Tranter kept hanging on the back of her bedroom door. Pressure with one end of the pole released the catch of the trapdoor. The hook on the other end of the same pole was for pulling down from the loft, through the open trapdoor, an extending metal ladder.

Brian insisted that he needed no help with toboggan, loft-pole, or loft-ladder. He could manage alone – he preferred to manage alone; Lenny and Kate could stay downstairs, watching their Laurel and Hardy.

Behind the sounds of the old film and of their own laughing at it, Kate heard Brian go upstairs and into their mother's room for the loft-pole. She heard him going up with it to the top landing. Then there was a silence: he must be fumbling with the loft-pole to get the trapdoor open. Then at last the familiar loud clang and clatter – that resounded through the whole house – as the metal loft-ladder was pulled down. Then again, silence: Brian must be climbing the ladder with the toboggan, taking it into the loft.

Brian was a long time in the loft – a very long time.

The Laurel and Hardy film came to an end, and Kate said: 'Do you think he's all right up there?'

'Brian?'

'He's been such a long time in the loft. He can't have suffocated. Or hit his head . . .'

'Silly . . .'

Just then they heard the distant din of the ladder going back into place, and, later, the sound of Brian's descending the stairs. He appeared before them, much dirtier than he had been before; he was brushing black cobwebs off his clothes. 'Well, I've put it away,' he said.

'The ladder worked all right?' asked Lenny.

'Yes. But your loft! – there's not much headroom: I had to creep about on all fours, almost. And so many things up there! I poked about a bit . . .'

So that was it! thought Kate. Not suffocated; not concussed; just inquisitive . . .

'There was a huge old fireguard. And a folding table, broken. Lots and lots of stuff. Who does it all belong to?'

'Us, of course,' said Lenny. 'Mum puts our spare stuff up there.'

'Oh,' said Brian. Then: 'There's a camp-bed, in a plastic bag. Rolls of wallpaper in a suitcase. There are some pillows, too. Would those all be your mum's?'

'Of course.'

'I just wondered . . .' For a moment Kate thought that Brian was going to say more; but he changed his mind. 'I just wondered,' he repeated.

With the toboggan, as well as the black tray, put away, and the snow vanished altogether, and even Lenny's ankle back to normal before long, the whole world seemed ordinary again to Kate – just as it had been before.

One thing was different though: Anna was Kate's friend. She began often to call at the house: she went upstairs with Kate to Kate's bedroom and saw Syrup on Kate's bed, and admired him and stroked him and tickled him; and he purred. Then Kate went to Anna's flat and saw her tabby cat and admired *him*. She stayed to tea. She liked having tea with Anna; but she still didn't like Anna's father. He tended to snap.

They withdrew to Anna's bedroom. This room, like all the rest of the flat, was very tidy and clean. 'He does it all himself, even my room,' said Anna. 'The whole flat. He won't let me help.'

'It's nice,' said Kate guardedly.

Anna studied her, sizing her up as a friend. 'Yes,' she said, 'but his cooking's awful. I don't know why. It's better when we just eat straight out of tins.'

Kate said carefully, 'Your mum doesn't do much?'

'She's not here. She went off.'

'Oh?' said Kate, trying to understand and not seem stupid. 'She left?'

'She left. She left my dad; and she left *me*.'

Kate wanted to ask why, but this seemed too difficult.

'She got fed up,' said Anna airily. 'They're getting a divorce. Then I expect my dad will marry again.'

'Oh,' said Kate.

Anna said: 'Your mum's a widow, isn't she?'

'Yes,' said Kate, a step behind Anna in her thinking.

'Well,' said Anna, 'when my dad's got his divorce, he could marry your mum.' She laughed uproariously, to show that all this could be taken as a joke. Then she added: 'Then we'd be really close friends. We'd be sort of half-sisters. We'd live together. We could share the same bedroom, and have a cat on each bed.'

Kate was bewildered by the suddenness of the project. 'But – I mean, I don't think my mum wants to marry anyone.'

'Why not?' asked Anna. 'People often do. My dad would be a golden opportunity.'

'I'm not sure,' said Kate.

'Why not?' persisted Anna.

'I've got to go home now,' said Kate. The conversation appalled her. The possibility of her mother's re-marrying – well, it was an impossibility. What about Granny, for one thing?

Kate went straight home; and she was very cool with Anna at school next day, and did not let her enter the house for the whole of that week. Kate's mother noticed, and asked: 'Where's Anna?'

'I don't like her as much as I did,' said Kate.

'Tiffs,' said Mrs Tranter indulgently. Kate withdrew upstairs: hers seemed a thankless life.

Whenever Kate met Anna at school nowadays, she was afraid that Anna would resume the subject of parents' re-marrying; but Anna did not, after all. At last, Kate stopped being nervous of the possibility. She became at ease with Anna again. They were still friends.

Meanwhile, Shrove Tuesday was coming – a holiday for everyone. For Ipston, although not a town of great size or importance, prided itself on being itself, like no other town, and anciently had decided that Shrove Tuesday should be kept a general holiday.

Kate asked Anna to come to her house for pancakes at teatime, and Anna agreed. Lenny was there. Randall did not turn up until the pancakes were almost finished.

Everyone (except the cook) had had at least two pancakes – even old Mrs Randall had had one after another carried to her in her room. The kitchen table was now littered with squashed lemon halves and sugar messes and empty plates. Mrs Tranter was hot and tired, but pleased with herself. 'I think I'll make *my* second pancake now,' she said.

Randall, who was standing in the kitchen doorway, looking at them all, said: 'I'll do you one, Mum.'

'Don't be silly, Ran. You can't.'

'Oh, yes, I can! I've been taking lessons. You'll see.'

He pressed her down into the empty chair, and she let him.

'My dad can't make pancakes,' said Anna. 'He tried once. His end up all lumpy – too thick where they're lumpy and too thin everywhere else.'

'He gets the batter wrong,' said Mrs Tranter.

They all watched Ran as he re-greased the pan, then turned the gas up under it. He poured most of the remaining batter-mixture in, with great splutterings, then spent time loosening the edges of the pancake from the sides of the pan, using his cooking knife. He began wriggling the pan to make sure that the pancake moved freely in it.

'You're surely not going to try tossing it!' cried Mrs Tranter.

'I am.' He held the pan out straight in front of him, using both hands. Then he swivelled round, to turn his back upon them all.

'We can't see!' said Lenny.

'Not meant to,' said Ran. Then Kate – who was nearest to him – heard him count under his breath: 'One – two – three!' On 'three!' she saw his whole body jerk, and the pancake jumped from the pan, not soaring, but high enough for everyone to see – 'Hurrah!' shouted Lenny – and it turned over in mid-air, and fell back flat into the pan again with a little slap.

The pan went back on to the gas for less than a minute, and then the pancake was done. Ran slithered it on to his mother's plate: 'There!'

There was still a little batter left. 'Just enough for two midget pancakes,' said Ran. So he made a tiny pancake each for Kate and Anna.

'But you haven't had one yourself, Ran,' said Mrs Tranter.

'I don't need one,' said Ran, and smiled. Kate saw the

smile, and could imagine Ran and Vicky, earlier that very afternoon, tossing pancakes and eating them in Vicky's mother's kitchen, while – perhaps from the next room – there came the sound of Ran's record player.

Kate saw Anna looking at Ran, admiring him. She felt very friendly towards Anna. She thought: When I have my birthday, in the summer, I'll ask Anna. Then she thought: And I'll do something special with her on my birthday. I'll take her to see my father's tombstone and the date on it – the date of that very day, my birthday.

Then she thought: Why wait?

The pancake party was quite over: Mrs Tranter had started the washing up. Ran went upstairs to work. Lenny went to fetch some piece of equipment from Brian. Mrs Tranter said to Kate and Anna: 'Well, now, you two, are you going to watch TV with the cat?'

Anna opened her mouth to answer, but Kate said: 'I think we'll go for a walk.'

Mrs Tranter glanced at the window: 'It'll be getting dark soon ...'

'A short walk,' said Kate.

'Where to?' asked her mother; but Kate pretended not to have heard. She hurried Anna out of the house.

As they went off together, Kate said to Anna, 'You're my friend, and I'm going to show you something special – something extraordinary.' She would stand with Anna in front of her father's tombstone, and point to the date on it – the date of her own birth. Nobody knew that Kate knew about that tombstone. But, after today, her friend, Anna, would know.

'What is it? What *is* it?' Anna was asking.

'Wait,' said Kate.

They turned in at the churchyard gate, and Kate led the way towards the corner she knew so well. From a distance she could already see, on one side, the toddler-angel on its plinth, and, on the other, the white stone cross. And now, between the two, she could see –

'What is it, then?' asked Anna.

They were standing exactly where Kate had intended, and Kate was staring. Anna peered all round her; and, at last, she peered into Kate's face. 'What is it, Cath? Why do you look like that?'

Kate did not answer, but stared and stared. There, in front of them, between the angel and the cross, was a space. There was the usual shallow grassy mound, about the length of a man and the width of a man. But there was no headstone with inscription.

The tombstone had gone.

Chapter 6

OTHER PEOPLE; OTHER PLACES

From the churchyard Anna had to go home alone to her flat; and she did not believe – never could believe – that Kate had really taken her on that expedition to see only a miserable runt of a stone angel. For this was all that Anna had been able to make out from the jumbled excuses Kate had offered, after that first long, stunned silence. What had become plain to Anna, however, was Kate's wish to be alone.

Kate flew home alone through the gathering dusk, her feet winged with amazement and fear. She must tell someone (but never Anna) of what – impossibly – had happened; she must share and thereby lessen the terrifying strangeness of such a disappearance.

She was almost home before she began to wonder whom she should tell.

Oddly (when she considered afterwards), the first person to come into her mind was her grandmother. She remembered the sight of her grandmother standing before the tombstone among the falling snowflakes and lifting her stick towards the stone. Granny knew all about it; and undoubtedly she knew many things that Kate did not. If Kate rushed into her room and knelt by her side and seized her knobbly old hands and told her what had happened and begged and begged her to explain ...

Kate opened the front door and walked just inside and stood there, panting, between the door and the beam of darkness. She turned slowly towards that beam. She nerved herself to do what she had imagined herself as doing; but –

No. She could not.

Neither could she go to her mother. Her mother would not like her to have been in a churchyard, at dusk, looking at tombstones. Would she consent to listen to her story? And if she did, would her mother not say all this was nonsense, sick fancy? Kate must not take on so! All a mistake! – *Could* her mother say that? And if not, what would she say? She, who was the widow of the Alfred of the tombstone ... Oh, it was more than Kate's confused imagination could bear!

Then she decided: Ran. The memory of the tiny pancake – of the two tiny pancakes for Katy and her friend – decided her.

By now Ran was in his room, working at his books. She would not have dared to disturb him on any other day; and, on any other day, he would probably not have put up with the interruption. But today, after the pancake party, he smiled at her.

'Ran, I must tell you something.'

'All right. But be quick.'

She began at once, hurriedly and without plan, and very soon found herself floundering in her narrative. Already Ran was frowning. In fright, she took a short cut and said baldly: 'Our dad's tombstone in the churchyard – it's disappeared!'

Ran sighed. 'Oh, Kate . . .'

'Did you know he was buried in the churchyard – *here?*'

'No, I didn't. But I knew he must be buried somewhere. What does it matter?'

'It matters to me. I was born the day he died. There it was on his tombstone: ALFRED TRANTER, and the very date I was born – and the tombstone's gone!'

Ran said: 'You were born the day he died – yes. But the rest – Kate, you know you're inventing it all.'

'No, I'm not!'

'You're telling lies, Kate.'

'No!'

'Yes, Kate. Look!' He turned back to the table where he had been working with several text books open before him. He took one of them and flipped the pages back to the very beginning. He held the book so that Kate could see the inside of the cover, where he had written his name, as owner of the book:

R. F. TRANTER

He pointed to the first initial. 'R is for Randall, after our mum – her surname before she married.' He pointed to the second initial: 'F is for Frederick – after our dad.'

'Our dad's name was Fred.'

'Yes. Short for Frederick.'

'No! You're wrong, Ran! It was Alfred – it must have been Alfred – Alfred was on the tombstone. It was – it was!'

Ran said: 'You knew our dad was called Fred, and you decided that his full name must have been Alfred, and the next thing is you think you see a tombstone with ALFRED TRANTER on it, and the next thing is you think the tombstone's vanished, although it was never there in the first place.'

'No!' cried Kate.

But Ran swept on: 'It's all your mystery-making and rubbish. Like the business of that letter.'

'What letter?' said Kate, bewildered.

'The letter in purple ink that was delivered by hand for Granny, and she yelled out at it. You made a big song and dance to me at the time; and now you've just forgotten!'

That! said Kate. She remembered now – but with difficulty – what had happened before the great snow-fall.

'Yes, that – and now you're making another mystery out of nothing – *nothing!*'

'This is different,' Kate said earnestly. 'I've seen this tombstone – truly! I've seen it. I've touched it, Ran. And now it's vanished.'

Suddenly he lost all patience with her. He became furiously angry. 'What are you up to? What are you playing at? Our dad's dead, isn't he? What does it matter about his tombstone, you silly little girl?'

'But, Ran –'

'I tell you,' Ran almost shouted, 'I remember him! I remember what it was like when he was alive. You weren't born, and Lenny was too young; but I remember – just.'

'What was it like?' breathed Kate.

'I remember Dad; and he taught at the school where I'd just started. I must have been five. And there was an Uncle Bob –'

'An Uncle Bob?'

'*Don't interrupt.* He was Dad's brother. They used to fool around sometimes and play with me, and Mum used to laugh at us. They used to take me down to Sattin Shore to paddle and make mud-pies.'

'Where's –'

'*Shut up.* About that time, something awful happened

54

on Sattin Shore. Someone drowned.' He stopped speaking, but only because he was trying to say the next thing. 'There was an awful muddle. Mum went off in an ambulance to the hospital because she was having you, and Granny came and took Lenny and me and brought us here to her house in Ipston, and we've all lived here ever since. It was Granny that told me that Dad had drowned.'

Kate clutched at almost the last thing that Ran had said. 'You mean, we haven't always lived here?'

But Ran just said: 'I've told you – I've told you all I know – all I remember. I don't want to talk about it any more – ever. Now go! I want to work. Get out! Go! And don't come back!'

Kate left Randall's room. She stood on the little landing outside and leaned against the wall, trying to steady her mind.

Of course, she knew that there had been another time – a time before she was born. There were other places; other people, too. Ran, her own brother, partly belonged to those other places and those people; and, as for her mother and her grandmother – she was afraid when she peered backwards into the darkness of the times they had known.

All that was bad enough, without thinking of the tombstone and what Ran had said about it – and about her. She would not think of that at all.

Other people; other places ...

Uncle Bob; Sattin Shore ...

She forced herself to concentrate, to begin with, on this Uncle Bob. As far as she had ever known – but she had never particularly bothered to ask – her only family were the people who lived here in this house: mother, grandmother, brothers ... No aunts, uncles, cousins.

Yet they had not always lived in this house, Ran said. Another house, other people. Among them, Uncle Bob . . .

And Sattin Shore?

She'd never heard of Sattin Shore. Every summer the Tranter family – without old Mrs Randall, who managed with some outside help for that week – went off to the seaside at Sandby. (Last summer Ran had refused to go, and remained at home instead.) They went by coach and stayed always in the same boarding house. There was a shore at Sandby, of course, but it was simply called The Beach. On different occasions they had walked along the shore for a considerable way. In one direction they had walked almost as far as the sandy spit called the Ness. In the other direction they had walked to within sight of the next little resort along the coast, Seamouth. But no Sattin Shore . . .

No Uncle Bob; no Sattin Shore . . .

She had reached a dead end in her thinking; but, by thinking, she had at least managed to calm herself. By thinking, she had made herself better able to think.

She would ask Lenny.

When she knocked on his door, he called out, 'Wait!' There was the sound of curtains being drawn. Then, 'Come in!'

She opened the door: inside was deep darkness; the curtains now across the window had shut out the very last of daylight.

'Lenny?' She took a hesitant step forward into the room, and something brushed thinly against her extended hand, with a sudden sensation that was not exactly painful, but certainly was not pleasant. She felt what she had felt when riding on the Ghost Train at the Midsummer Fair.

She had given a little gasp at the stinging touch of whatever it was, and stepped back.

Lenny's voice – she could now just distinguish him crouching on the bed, with apparatus round him – said, 'Good!' in a satisfied tone. There was no animosity in it.

From the safety of the doorway, Kate said: 'I wanted to ask you something, Lenny.'

'Would you mind making contact again? I'm working on a sort of electric fence.'

'Lenny –'

'Just touch the live wire again.'

'But, Lenny –'

'Please, Kate!'

Bargain, then: 'I will, Lenny, if you'll talk to me first.'

'Talk to you?'

'I want to ask you two things. Then I'll touch your wire again.'

'Well?'

'Did you know we had an Uncle Bob?'

He considered. 'No. No, I didn't.'

'And where's Sattin Shore?'

'Never heard of it,' said Lenny. 'No.' Kate braced herself now to make the contact; but Lenny had not finished. 'Wait a minute. There's Sattin – a village. I biked through it once with Brian.'

'But Sattin Shore?'

'I don't know ...' He was puzzled.

'Not near Sandby or Seamouth?'

'Sattin wasn't anywhere near the sea. If it has a shore, it must be on the estuary. Yes, on the estuary. Now, will you make contact again, please, Kate?'

She wanted full value for her co-operation. 'Lenny, could you show me on a map?'

'Yes. Now – contact!'

She advanced again towards the wire and – almost before she touched it – gave a little scream. She thought Lenny would like that.

And, in a way, it was a relief to scream, even briefly.

Chapter 7

NOR CAT NOR RAT

In the time that followed, Kate sometimes said to herself: 'I shouldn't have to think as hard as this – not *think* – at my age.'

She had to hold so many things in her mind at once, so many possibilities – so many impossibilities, too. She had to try to arrange them, to rearrange them, fit them together like the pieces of a jigsaw puzzle, so that at last they might make a complete, sensible picture. They must make sense. They *must*.

Could a tombstone really vanish? Or was what Ran had said true – that the tombstone could not have vanished, because it had never been there in the first place? Had she invented something so solid and cold and stern? And had she invented, as he said, the inscription with ALFRED instead of FREDERICK? Had she really invented it all? She could not believe that: she had seen the tombstone with her own eyes, touched the lettering of the names upon it with her own fingers.

(The names: what was there at the back of her mind – of her memory – that made her feel afraid?)

And she had seen her mother and her grandmother

looking at the stone. Or had she? Could she be sure, at such distance, that those two figures had been her mother and grandmother? If they had been, then could she swear that they had stopped in front of that very tombstone – that her grandmother had lifted her stick to point to the names on that tombstone and no other?

(The names again; and again that quick, shadowy fear.)

When she fell asleep at night, her mind relaxed its usual hold, and another kind of weird thinking began. She stood in a fog on a satiny shore. The place was frightening. A shape was coming towards her through the fog. An upright, rather narrow shape. A man? No, an oblong thing – a tombstone came hopping towards her through the fog. The tombstone was calling out to her in her grandmother's voice: 'Look at this! Look – look!' She was afraid to look at the writing on the tombstone: she turned and ran, but her feet were weighed down, as so often in dreams, and she ran only slowly, so slowly ... Her grandmother's voice pursued her, now calling her by name: 'Alice Catharine Tranter, look at this! Look – look!' (How extraordinary for her grandmother to address Kate by all her names: nobody ever did that!)

As Kate ran along the satiny shore, jigsaw puzzles began to rain their pieces upon her head; and a voice distorted by laughter shouted: 'Bob's your uncle!' She looked back over her shoulder to see whoever it was: there was no one there. But she was just in time to see the tombstone vanish. Whatever else happened in the dream, the tombstone always vanished.

In the daytime, Kate did not like to remember what she had dreamed of at night. It seemed as if she were afraid to remember. Anyway, she decided not to think any more about the tombstone. It did no good; she simply would not. There were other parts of the puzzle, after all. What about Sattin Shore?

And this Uncle Bob? Why had no one, before Ran, ever spoken of him? Where had he been all these years? Where was he now? What could he tell her, perhaps?

At school she was accused of daydreaming instead of listening to the teacher; and Anna, who sat next to her at their double desk, pestered her.

They were doing a test-paper. Kate had written her name as usual at the top: Catharine Tranter. But no, she saw that she had written all her names: Alice Catharine Tranter.

(All her names, as in the dream; and that made her afraid.)

The children did the test. Then they exchanged papers, and began marking each other's answers. Anna had got most of her answers right; Kate had got most of her answers wrong. Kate had certainly not been listening properly to Mr Porter.

'You've been so *silly*,' Anna said disgustedly. 'And what's *that*?' She pointed indignantly to the top of Kate's paper.

'My name – my names.'

'Isn't Catharine your first name, then?'

'No.'

'That's stupid. It's the name you're called by. It's the name that matters. Why doesn't Catharine come first?'

Kate did not reply: she knew the answer to that question, but she was afraid to say it, even to herself, because she foresaw some shadowy thing that would try to follow in her thinking.

'Why aren't you Catharine Alice Tranter?' persisted Anna. 'Why?' Then she began to giggle. 'But I see why!'

'No!' said Kate. She did not want her thinking to go that way. She would have to face a thing she did not want to face. She would have to make up her mind to it . . .

Anna was saying: '– Because your initials would be C.A.T. – they'd spell "cat"!'

In Kate's mind, suddenly, the tombstone was there: she was looking full at it: she was reading the names on it: ALFRED ROBERT TRANTER. The name that mattered was not Alfred, after all, but Robert. The reason that Robert did not come first was clear: Robert Alfred Tranter would have spelt 'rat'.

'And you're like a cat sometimes, Cathy Tranter,' Anna was saying. 'You're friendly one minute, and the next you go off all by yourself and have secrets.'

Robert Tranter – so that was where Uncle Bob had been all these years! He would never tell her anything. There he lay silent forever in the churchyard – as they say, silent as the grave.

Uncle Bob was buried there; not her father, after all.

Then –

Then –

Then, where was her father? Where was the Frederick Tranter who had *not* – after all – died on the day she had been born? If he were not in the churchyard, where was he?

Alive? *Alive?*

She stood up suddenly from her desk, confused by the upheaval in her own mind.

'Cathy Tranter, what are you doing now?' asked Mr Porter.

'Nothing, please. Please, I don't think I feel very well.'

'Sick?' Mr Porter was instantly alert.

'No.' She sat down again. 'I'm all right, really.'

'Make your mind up,' said Mr Porter. He turned to his blackboard again. Kate looked at the back of him and thought: 'He might be anybody, from the back. When you see his face, he's Mr Porter. But, from the back, he might be anybody ... Anybody, from the back, might be my father. Anybody I don't know might be my father. Because – should I ever recognize my own father? Where is he now? *Who* is he?'

Mr Porter swung round from the blackboard, perhaps with the intention of catching one of his pupils in some unacceptable act. He caught Cathy Tranter looking at him in a way he did not like.

'And what are you staring at?'

'Nobody,' said Kate, when, of course, she ought to have said, 'Nothing.' She saw her mistake: 'I – I mean, I can see now that you're nobody –'

This made things worse. The other children ducked their heads to laugh. Mr Porter, strongly suspecting impertinence, frowned: 'I warn you, Catharine!' he said. (Against what? Against *whom*?) 'I'm just warning you!'

For the rest of Kate's school day, and on the way home, the back of every man she saw seemed as if it might be the back of her father. In the end, she was running home, with her head down, afraid of whom she might see.

She burst into the house and stood just inside the front door.

Two unusual things: her grandmother's door was shut; and there was a sound of movement from the kitchen. Then she remembered: this was her mother's half day from the confectionery where she worked. She was home early. She often cooked on her free afternoon – she liked cooking, anyway.

The resolution was already in Kate's mind to talk to her mother at last, however difficult that might be. She would tell her everything – always excepting Ran's part of the story, which was private to him. She would tell her mother about the disappearing tombstone; she would ask why Uncle Bob, and not her father, had died on the day she was born – or rather, she would ask why she had not been told the truth. She would ask where her father was now. That last above all.

She went into the kitchen.

Her mother was making pastry. She stood at the kitchen table over the big mixing bowl, rubbing the fat into the flour between the tips of downward-pointing fingers. As she rubbed, the dry pastry mixture scattered down on to the heap in the bowl. When the last crumbs of the mixture had fallen, she dipped her hands into the heap and raised just enough again to rub-rub-rub and scatter-scatter-scatter and then *dip* and again rub-rub-rub and scatter-scatter-scatter and *dip* and rub-rub-rub –

And on the other side of the kitchen table sat Kate's grandmother, watching intently.

So that was why her grandmother's door had been shut! When Mrs Tranter did any long job in the kitchen, old Mrs Randall often joined her there. They talked sometimes.

Her mother and her grandmother both turned their heads to look at Kate for a moment. Mrs Tranter did not stop rubbing, but she said: 'You're the first back, Kate. When I've mixed this lot, I'll be making our teas.'

'Yes,' said Kate.

Her grandmother had gone back to her watching. Kate looked at her and willed her to say: 'Well, I've seen enough. I'll get back to my room now.' Or she might even say, 'Well, I'll leave you, Catharine, now that's Kate's home.'

She said neither thing. She went on watching the pastry being made.

Rub-rub-rub scatter-scatter-scatter *dip* rub-rub-rub scatter-scatter-scatter *dip* rub-rub-rub –

'Mum!' said Kate.

'Yes?' Mrs Tranter looked up from her rubbing. Old Mrs Randall also looked at Kate.

'Nothing,' said Kate.

Rub-rub-rub –

Kate took a step to the table, reached out and caught one of her mother's hands, so that the rubbing had to stop. She held her mother's floury hand between both of hers. They were looking into each other's eyes now. 'Mum,' said Kate. Then: 'Mum, it's true. Your hand's quite cold. You say you need cold hands for pastry.'

'Yes, I've cool hands.' Mrs Tranter spoke with the patience that is clearly seen to be on the edge of impatience. 'Now, Kate ...'

Kate still held her mother's hand between her own: 'Mum –'

Mrs Randall said, 'You're stopping your mother getting on with her work.'

Kate let go of her mother's hand. She swept her own hands together to get rid of the dusting of pastry-mixture. Her grandmother said, 'You're messing the floor, girl.'

The work had resumed: rub-rub-rub scatter-scatter-scatter *dip* rub-rub-rub scatter-scatter-scatter *dip* –

'Was there something?' asked Mrs Tranter.

'No,' said Kate. 'Well, have you seen Syrup?'

'Always that cat!' said Mrs Tranter. 'No.' Rub-rub-rub scatter-scatter-scatter *dip* rub-rub-rub –

'I expect he's upstairs,' said Kate. 'I'll go and see.'

At the kitchen door she paused to look back. Her mother and her grandmother were both looking at her again, waiting for her to go.

She closed the kitchen door behind her.

At that moment of disappointment – of a kind of explosive despair – the idea came into Kate's head that she would visit Sattin Shore. Not when summer came. Not when she had practised cycling longer distances. Not when she could persuade Lenny to come with her.

She would go by herself, tomorrow. She must do some-

thing about her father at once – immediately. Something
that mattered. Otherwise she felt as if she might burst
– explode and scatter into pieces.

Chapter 8

OUT OF SCHOOL

The one thing that might have made Kate alter her intention of going to Sattin Shore was the weather; but the morning after her decision shone bright with soft, spring sunshine. A cowardly part of her wished that it had been otherwise.

She set off from home as if cycling to school. She did not usually cycle to school, but she told her mother that she and Anna wanted to compare bicycles. Kate knew this sounded an unlikely story, but her mother – who was not a cyclist herself – smiled and nodded and seemed to accept what she was being told. Kate told her that she would go straight from school with Anna to Anna's flat, and have tea with her. So Kate might be quite late home.

Lies ... But they gave Kate cover for her expedition, and time. She had no idea how long her trip might last. She had no idea what might await her on Sattin Shore, or how long she might want to remain there. She had no idea, really, why she had to go there at all.

She cycled towards school at first, then veered off in order to leave the town in the direction of Gripe's Hill. She had committed herself now. She felt strange and free, as if she were cycling away from her own bewilderment and fears. She felt *light*. Light-hearted? No, not yet. Light-headed? Not exactly. Light-footed, certainly – her feet sent the pedals round almost without effort; the bicycle seemed to skim along. The speed of it delighted her.

But she was also nervous and watchful. She was still in a part of Ipston that she knew well – and that perhaps knew her. She recognized a greengrocer arranging his fruit on a pavement stand, and thought he must have noticed her. Further on, she saw people she knew on their way to work or to do early shopping. Somebody – an older girl – passed her swiftly on a bicycle and called, 'Hello!' but she wasn't even sure who it was. She wondered if anyone would send a message to the school: 'Should Catharine Tranter be cycling away from school on a school morning?'

Soon she was going through the outskirts of Ipston. There was much less bustle: a few women wheeling little children in prams and pushchairs; a street cleaner; a postman; delivery men getting in and out of their vans. Would they wonder at a girl of her age, on a school day, just cycling along?

A policeman . . .

But not even he paid any attention. And now the houses were newer – newly built in what had recently been countryside. And now the countryside was beginning: pavements became paths; walls or fences became hedge-rows, ditches.

Here was the country, and here, to one side of her, rose Gripe's Hill. It did not look as she remembered it. Neither as smooth and steep as in the snowy days of tobogganing, nor as richly turfed as on the days of summer picnics. Its slopes were mottled with thin spring greenness; the ways up and round the hill were still muddy with last winter's wet.

She would have liked to have gone on to Gripe's Hill again, but she was afraid of losing time. She cycled on. She knew that she was not very good at finding her way to places, but last night she had looked again at the map on which Lenny had shown her Sattin and, beyond it, the estuary and its shores. She had memorized the direction to take and the names of the villages to be passed through, one by one, on the way. And now here they came, one by one, memorized name after memorized name. She was on the right road; and she was surely making good time.

Then Sattin was the next village, and it was not yet midday. On the other hand, her legs had begun to tire from the pedalling. She wondered what they would feel like before the end of the day, if they felt tired now, before she had completed even half her expedition. She began to wonder, and then stopped; no use frightening herself.

She decided to take a rest before Sattin itself; and she might as well eat her lunch – her packed lunch, that was really for school. She wanted to stretch herself out and lie on the grass verge in the sun; but, when she tried, the grass at once struck cold through her clothing, and the ground felt squelchy. In the end she found the remains of some tree that had been felled a long time ago. She sat on the trunk and ate her lunch, but the seat wasn't comfortable – or restful.

She had nothing to drink with her lunch; at school, there would have been jugs of water along the tables. She supposed that she would have to buy a can or bottle of something in Sattin. She had brought some money with her, for emergencies.

The tree trunk was so uncomfortable that she soon went back to her bicycle, and cycled on into the village of Sattin. It was a very small village that – as the years passed – had been getting smaller. She cycled over what must once have been a level crossing at a railway station, but the station building was closed and even the railway lines had gone. In the one main street there were two shops, but the windows of one were boarded up. The other was a general store. She went in and bought a little bottle of fizzy lemonade. The shopkeeper opened it for her to drink there and then. She asked him the way down to Sattin Shore, for that was something she had not been able to understand from the map.

The shopkeeper told her: 'Go on to the old school. You'll know it by the clock. Turn just beyond the school. But the shore's still a fair way to go, after that.'

Hesitantly she asked: 'Will there be a tea-place?' She was thinking of the beach at Sandby, and yet already this place was so different.

The shopkeeper laughed. 'Nothing. Just fields and fields going down to the shore. No one lives there. Nothing.'

He made her feel ashamed of her ignorance. She was glad to leave the shop and go on.

The old school turned out to be a little, crouching building of dark red brick. In the gable end was a clock with a blank, hand-less face. Otherwise the school did not look derelict, but neither did it look like a school any more. Next to the school stood a little house built in exactly the same style, perhaps at the same time. The headmaster or headmistress might have lived there, Kate thought; and then remembered Ran's saying of their father: 'He taught there . . .'

Kate was still looking thoughtfully at the school building, when the figure of an old woman straightened itself in the front garden of another cottage, on the other side of the school.

She looked at Kate curiously – too curiously, Kate thought. And she seemed as if she might be going to speak: yes –

'It's a fine day,' said the old woman.

'Yes,' said Kate. 'Was that the school?'

'That's right, dear,' said the old woman.

'Not any longer?'

'In the end there were too few children. The school was shut down. It's someone's holiday house now.' Evidently the old woman was not used to the treat of seeing strangers. She looked at Kate even more closely, and made a remark of the kind that Kate had been dreading: 'Enjoying a day off from school?'

'Yes,' said Kate. 'It's – it's a special holiday.'

'Come far?' (So gentle, and so nosey!)

'From –' (but oughtn't she to be covering her tracks?) '– from beyond Ipston.'

'Ipston. I used to know Ipston well. Once.'

(So don't ask her any more about the Sattin school and who taught there. For she won't know, probably, and she'll only grow suspicious.)

The old woman was still staring at her. 'What's your name?'

(So perhaps she suspected something already! Quickly – *think*!) 'My name?' said Kate. 'I'm Anna Johnson.'

'I just wondered, dear,' said the old woman, suddenly humble again.

'Well,' said Kate, 'I must be getting on. I'm going to Sattin Shore. This is the way, isn't it?'

'Yes.' The old woman pointed to a turning a little further on. Then: 'What do you want, right down there?'

'I just want to see,' said Kate. 'You can bathe there, can't you?'

'Don't you go trying that,' said the old woman. 'Freezing cold the water will be still. And when it's warmer, you want to take care.'

'I can swim,' said Kate.

'So they all say, and then one drowns,' said the old woman.

'This way, then?' said Kate, gently getting her bicycle into motion.

'That's it. But you take care!' the old woman called after her. Then she went back to her weeding. Kate went on.

The turning, down a wide farm track, was just beyond the school buildings. There was no gate at the entrance to the track, but a notice board said: FOOTPATH ONLY, EXCEPT FOR ACCESS. NO CARS. The notice did not say where the footpath led, or what the access was to. Nor did it prohibit bicycles, and that gave Kate confidence.

She began cycling down the track, keeping to one of the ruts made most recently by a tractor. Every so often the rut widened into a shallow puddle, stretching almost across the way. Sometimes she had to ride through the water, feeling it splash muddily up her legs as she went.

On both sides of her, apple-orchards stretched ahead as well as back towards the road she had just left – or, at least, to meet the back gardens of the houses by the old school. The fruit trees grew in exactly straight diagonals, and all the time, as she cycled along by the orchards, she had new views down their avenues. At the end of these vistas, she began to see a long, low farmhouse, in front of which was parked a white van. Then she came to a drive with a gate across it, that bore the notice: SATTIN HALL FRUITFARM LTD. An angry little terrier came racing to the gate to bark at her. A man who seemed to be pruning the fruit trees peered at her from one of the avenues.

But Kate's track passed the fruitfarm and went on. The orchards gave way to open fields, with straight green lines of spring growth across them. In the landscape there was no change to suggest that she might be approaching the shores of an estuary.

She rode steadily along the track, which became no better and no worse. Further and further she went, until she found herself wondering whether the shopkeeper and the old weeding woman had both been tricking her. For there was not the slightest sign of her coming to Sattin Shore.

Suddenly the track came to an end. It simply broadened out into a flatness where tractors and other wheeled vehicles could turn – and had often done so. Ahead, there was no track at all: only a sharply rising bank with shrubs and stunted trees growing sparsely along its sides and top.

So this was where the track led: nowhere. All the light-heartedness, carefreeness of this stolen day of escape left her. She felt heavy, grey, stupid.

Yet she felt obstinate, too. She sat on her bicycle, her toes on the ground, balancing her, and stared round her. She searched the bank ahead with her eyes, and saw what might have been a path last summer. Feet had once marked a way there.

There was nowhere to lean her bicycle, so she laid it flat on the ground. Then she made for the faint path before her. She clambered up it, grasping at stems and branches to help her as she went. She broke through the scrub at the top of the bank and stood upright.

She gazed, dazzled. At her very feet lay Sattin Shore and the wide, gleaming waters of the estuary.

She looked and looked; and then she slid down the few feet of bank on to the shore itself. The surface was very stony, over ground that seemed half sand, half muddy earth. The tide in from the sea must be at the full, for as she looked in either direction, she could see that the width of the shore was nowhere more than about ten feet, in some places less. In some places the scrub and grass grew almost to the water's edge; and the coarser grass – or perhaps it was a kind of reed – actually grew out into the water.

She looked right across the estuary to the other side. She could see, in the furthest distance, houses here and there among trees. No people; but perhaps the distance was too great for her to distinguish people. There were no people visible anywhere, on that side or this. No other creatures, except for seagulls that must have come up from the coast, and now wheeled and skimmed far away, overhead, ignoring her.

She went to the water's edge, until her toes were almost rippled by it. She crouched down and dipped her fingers in the water, then her whole hand. As the old woman had said, the water was very, very cold. All the same, she held her hand under the surface, watching her fingers as she moved them fishily to and fro. Then she withdrew her hand and shook the water from it and dried it on her clothing; but her fingers were still numb with cold. She held them, for comfort, in her dry, warm other hand; and the cold hand felt even colder than her mother's when she made pastry. Then she held them under her armpit, as Ran had once taught her to do, and that began to warm them.

She stood upright again, and started to wander along the shore. The afternoon was still bright. No mist was creeping in from anywhere. No tombstone hopped. No voices called. There was nothing in the least alarming.

There was nobody. But people did sometimes come here, for here was a cigarette butt, and further on a dirty, tattered plastic bag – but that could have been on the shore for years.

She came to a whole, stubby tree, uprooted – probably from the bank – and lying with its crown in the water.

Long ago it had been denuded of leaves and twigs and most of its bark. She seated herself astride the trunk, looking across the estuary. This was the second tree she had sat on that day: the first had been at midday; now she observed that the sun was towards the west.

She listened to the occasional gull-cry, and to the sound of the wind in the trees of the bank behind her. Once she thought she heard a car engine, but she listened again more carefully, and there was nothing but the wind.

Then, out of the corner of her eye, she saw a movement in the direction from which she had come. She turned her head quickly and saw a dog – black and white, and terrier-like. It looked like the dog who had barked at the orchard gate. It came running down the bank and then stood on the shore, as if waiting for someone to follow.

Instantly Kate was afraid. She remembered her mother's warnings against being found alone in lonely places.

The dog had not yet seen her or scented her. She slipped from her tree-seat and moved swiftly across the strip of shore to the bank and its cover. From behind a bush, she watched.

A figure had appeared, following the dog. She was almost certain this was the man she had seen pruning in the orchard; if so, she had been right about the dog, in the first place. The man had binoculars slung round his neck. He stood by his dog, and raised his binoculars to his eyes and looked first one way and then the other along the shore. Then he began to walk unhurriedly along the shore in the direction she had taken. She could not be certain that he had glanced down and seen her newly made footprints in the soft ground at the water's edge, and she could not be certain that he had *not* done so.

She did not wait. She turned and went directly up the

bank at the point where she had taken cover. There was no path here, and she had to force her way through scrub that tore at her clothes and the skin of her face and hands. Several times she slipped and fell on all fours, and became like a frightened little animal scuttling in terror on the off-chance of danger. The bank seemed to stretch endlessly up; and then she found herself so suddenly at the top that she pitched forward on to the earth of the ploughed field on the other side.

She got up and began to run clumsily back in the direction of her bicycle – clumsily, because soft earth from the field had at once caked on her shoes, adding thickness and heavy weight. Yet she had to make the effort of moving quietly, so that the man on the shore would not hear her. She could only guess when, invisibly, they would be passing each other, she going in one direction, he in the other.

At last she reached the open spaces where she had left her bicycle – and there it was, just beside a white van along whose side was stencilled SATTIN HALL FRUITFARM LTD.

She examined her bicycle briefly – suppose one of the tyres was now down? All was well. She mounted and prepared to ride away. But she found that her feet, still clogged with wet earth, could not control the pedals. She must stop again to scrape off at least some of the mud. At first she worked with a wayside stone; then – as this seemed so slow – with her bare hands. Her hands trembled as they tore and scraped.

She rode off, at last. She feared to hear the van start up behind her; but it did not. She passed the gate of Sattin Hall Fruitfarm, and there was still no pursuit.

But then, why should there have been? Most reasonably, she told herself that the man with the binoculars had just gone to the shore with his dog for a stroll. He had not interfered with her bicycle, after all. He had not even waited by it, to be sure of catching her.

Catching her?

She was glad to be on her way home.

She passed the school and the schoolhouse and the cottage. The old woman had gone indoors, no doubt to make her tea. The afternoon would be coming to an end soon, although there was still plenty of daylight. There needed to be: Kate had a long way to go to get home.

She left the village of Sattin behind her, and now she was cycling back the way she had come in the morning. So the names of the villages were appearing in reverse order: that confused her tired mind. Her mind was tired; and, even more, her body was tired, and suffering from unusual discomforts. Mud was still thick on her feet, and on her hands. She was splashed from the puddles along the rutted track to the shore. Her hair had been tangled and pulled during that stealthy rush up the bank from the shore. The same rush had caused grazes, scratches, cuts; and she was bruised from her fall to the ground on the other side of the bank.

And now rain began to fall – only a light spring drizzle, but she hated the wetness on her face. She kept her head down as she cycled, for as long as the shower lasted.

That made her lose her way: head down, looking around as little as possible, she took a wrong turning. She realized her mistake only when the names of the villages began to be unfamiliar, wrong.

Still she cycled despairingly on for some time, then asked her way, and was given directions for Ipston. Yes, she was off the correct route by several miles.

She reached the right road again; but she was tired – so tired.

She cycled on.

She saw a telephone box. Its redness stopped her. She

got off her bicycle and stood, leaning across it, to rest her back and shoulders: she wanted to think something out. If they had a telephone at home, and if she had the right change in her pocket, then she could telephone home, and her mother would answer the telephone, and she – Kate – could tell her where she was, and how tired she was. And if her mother had a car, and could drive it, she would come in the car and pick her – Kate – up. The bicycle would go inside the car – which would have to be rather a large one – or on to a roof-rack.

She thought all that, carefully; and then she realized that none of it helped, because none of it was true, and she must get home by herself on her bicycle. She began quietly to cry. This was the very moment when, in stories, someone – it would have to be someone she knew, such as Mr Porter, or that greengrocer, or the vicar – when someone came by in a car and gave her a lift home. But no one came by, so in the end she stopped crying and got on to her bicycle again and pedalled off, even more slowly than before. But she pedalled and pedalled and pedalled and pedalled . . .

And at long, long last, just before lighting-up time, she got home.

Chapter 9

MRS RANDALL CLIMBS THE STAIRS

Kate pushed her bicycle into the house and let it fall, a dead thing, against the wall of the back passage. Then she walked stiffly into the kitchen, past her mother, to the sink. She filled herself a mug of water from the tap and began to drink it, slowly. She might drink another after that. And another.

Looking at her state, Mrs Tranter said: 'What *have* you and Anna been up to?'

'Me and Anna?' Kate was confused. Then the memory came back to her of the morning of that very day and what she had told her mother then. 'Oh, me and Anna – yes ... Our bikes ... Yes, we biked about a bit ... Exploring, and – well ...' She was too tired to go on.

'First thing you need is a bath,' said Mrs Tranter. 'And take those shoes off before you go upstairs.'

In the bath, Kate had hardly enough energy to wash herself clean. When she had done as much as she knew she must, she lay back in the hot bathwater, put the bar of soap on her stomach, and stared at it. She gently arched and then straightened her back as she lay there, to send

ripples of bathwater up to the soap and over it ... Up
and over ... Up and over ...

She yawned deeply, on the point, it seemed, of rocking
herself to sleep.

The front door bell rang, far away and nothing to do
with her. Kate heard feet going across the hall: her
mother. The door was opened, and there were voices in
conversation. One voice was her mother's, of course; the
other – light, almost inaudible, perhaps familiar – yes,
certainly so: Anna.

Anna!

Kate sat up in the bath so suddenly that the displaced
water surged in a wave that snatched the soap with it.
Before the water had settled to a smooth surface – before
the front door had shut again – Kate had left bath and
bathroom and was in her own bedroom, more or less
towelled dry, and in her nightdress. She rushed into
bed.

Her mother called from below: 'Come down, Kate!'

Kate called back: 'I'm in bed.' Added, 'I'm nearly asleep.'
She cowered under the duvet.

There was no answer to that, but she heard her mother
coming upstairs. Mrs Tranter walked into the bedroom
to the foot of the bed, and stood there. She said: 'You
never went with Anna at all. You never went to school
at all. What have you been up to? You come home covered
with dirt; hair all over the place; scratched, bruised.
Kate, what have you been doing? Where have you
been?'

Kate said faintly: 'I went a long bike ride.'

'Who with?'

'No one.'

'Where did you go?'

'I went to Sattin Shore.'

'You went to Sattin Shore ...'

Mrs Tranter stared at her daughter; Kate stared back. Neither spoke.

The bedroom door had been left wide open at the time of Mrs Tranter's entry. In the doorway, Syrup now appeared. He walked delicately across the floor, right up to the bed, and jumped on to the duvet. He settled down. His purring, when it began, sounded loud in the quietness of the room.

'Sattin Shore,' said Mrs Tranter at last. 'I didn't know you knew such a place existed.'

'Ran told me, and Lenny.'

'You went there all by yourself?'

'Yes.'

'Why did you go?'

'I just wanted to see it.'

'What did you do when you got there?'

'I just walked along the shore, and looked.'

'You didn't meet anyone there? You didn't talk to anyone?'

'No.' After all, she had hardly *met* the man with the dog.

'You're sure you didn't talk to anyone on Sattin Shore or in Sattin – in the village, I mean?'

'No. Honestly.'

There was a pause, as if at the end of a conversation. Then Mrs Tranter said, 'I don't want you to go there again, Kate. Ever.'

'But, Mum, why not?'

'Never you mind why not!' And Mrs Tranter turned on her heel to march out of the bedroom.

Such a departure takes only a few short seconds; but Kate had time to feel a long despair. She felt it here and now; and it seemed always to have been lying in wait for her; and she saw it ahead of her, stretching before her like a long, long road, like the rest of her life . . .

She had wanted to talk to her mother when her mother had been making pastry, and she had not been able to. Now she could have done: she had her mother all to herself – and her mother was going. She would not wait. She would not listen.

Despair told Kate that if she did not seize her chance now, it would not come again. And she was too tired to seize it: she was too tired to prevent her mother's going, to make her stay and listen. Her will was too tired.

Feebly Kate began to cry, with no sound in her crying. The room was silent except for the noise of Mrs Tranter's going. Syrup had stopped purring.

In the very doorway of the bedroom, Mrs Tranter paused – she could not have said why. She listened to the silence behind her, and was disturbed by it. She turned her head, looked back over her shoulder at Kate. She saw Kate sitting up in bed, with despairing eyes from which the tears streamed without ceasing.

Mrs Tranter went back to the bed, leaned over it and took Kate in her arms: 'Katy, what is it?'

Kate clutched at her mother; but she still could not say the things she had to say.

'Katy, you must tell me . . .'

'Mum . . .' She wept and wept. 'I'm so hungry. I didn't have any tea . . .'

Her mother said: 'I'll get you something to eat.' And at her mother's words, Kate wept more than ever, because what she – Kate – had said was not at all what she needed to say. Not at all.

Mrs Tranter said gently: 'And is that all?'

'No . . .'

'What else is there?'

But Kate could not speak for tears.

'Anyway, I'll get you something.' Mrs Tranter was not gone long. She came back carrying a steaming bowl of bread and milk, and a spoon to eat it with. Nobody had bread and milk nowadays, Kate knew, except her grandmother; but Mrs Tranter used to make it sometimes if one of her children were not well. The milk had to be very hot, but not boiled; the bread torn up into small fragments; and there must be a little salt and a little nutmeg and a lot – oh! a lot – of sugar, the kind that came in coarse, Syrup-coloured crystals.

Her mother gave her the bowl and spoon and then went out again – 'just for a minute'. She came back with the electric blow-heater that she kept in her own bedroom. She plugged it in. Then she shut the door. Then she drew the curtains close. Then she switched off the light, so that the room was in darkness for a moment, and Kate stopped eating her bread and milk. But then Mrs Tranter turned the heater on: besides blowing out hot air, it gave a red glow to the room. Kate knew perfectly well that the red glow came only from a red-painted electric light bulb inside the fire; but that made no difference. She and her mother were shut into a safe, warm, reddish gloom of light. She could just see to eat her bread and milk. She could just see the dark shape of her mother, sitting on the edge of the bed, close to her. Against one of Kate's legs lay a heavy weight of contentment: the dozing Syrup.

Kate spooned up her bread and milk, not crying any more; and the dark shape of her mother watched her, patiently waiting.

From below came Lenny's voice: 'Mum!'

Mrs Tranter never moved.

Again, 'Mum!'

Mrs Tranter got up, went to the bedroom door, and opened it a little. 'What is it, Lenny?'

'Granny wants you.'

'I know she does. Tell her I'll be down later. I'm with Kate. She's not well.'

'All right.'

'And, Lenny –'

'Yes?'

'Don't call again. I'll be down as soon as I can.'

Mrs Tranter shut the door and came back to the bed and sat down again.

Kate had finished her bread and milk. Her mother took the bowl and spoon from her and put it aside. Now they faced each other; but in that warm dusk neither could see the other's face clearly. It was easier for them, so.

'Now, Katy ...'

Kate locked her fingers together and looked down at them. She opened her mouth to speak, and wondered what words would come out. But she began at once.

First of all, out came her terror at the disappearance of the tombstone that had recorded, on the very date of her own birth, the death of her father – but no! not her father's death, after all, but her uncle's – And who was this Uncle Bob? And where was her father then, if he were not there in the churchyard? Alive? But nowhere? – As the tombstone was nowhere? Vanished as absolutely as the tombstone?

Kate came back to her beginning, with the vanishing tombstone; and the tombstone was what Mrs Tranter began with.

'It hasn't vanished, Kate. The memorial masons took it away – the people who make tombstones and carve the writing on them. Your grandmother and I asked the masons to take the stone back to their yard, to carve another inscription on it. There was already Grandfather Tranter's name and the date of his death. There was his elder son's name – your Uncle Bob – and the date of *his* death. You know all that. Those two Tranters are buried there. And now your grandmother has asked the masons

to add the name of your father and the date of his death
– although he's not actually buried there.'

'So my dad is dead?'

'Yes, he died abroad. He didn't die on the very day
you were born, although we let you all think so: it seemed
better that way –'

Kate had opened her mouth to ask, Why – why *better*
to pretend, to lie about her father?

But her mother hurried on: 'It was Bob who died that
day, drowned on Sattin Shore. Your father went abroad.
He died abroad, later. A little later. Word came to your
grandmother – to us both – of his having died. We decided
to get his name put on the tombstone. In memory of
him …'

It was too dark for Kate to see the expression on her
mother's face, but something moved there, and glittered.
She had never seen her mother cry before.

'But, Mum …' she said, trying to think out all the
things she still needed to know. Why had they lied to
her about her father? Her father had died 'later – a little
later'; but when? And where? And how had he come to
die?

And what about Sattin Shore?

'Mum, tell me –'

But her mother was not listening to her now. Instead,
she was listening to a sound that came from outside the
room: a recurring thump and shuffle of someone slowly,
heavily climbing the stairs.

They were both listening now.

'No!' said Mrs Tranter under her breath. 'It can't
be …'

The climbing footsteps reached Kate's door. The door
was opened. Someone's hand fumbled along the wall just
inside for the light switch. The light went on.

Kate and her mother, screwing up their eyes against

the sudden light, saw the figure of old Mrs Randall in the doorway.

'Well?' she said. 'Well?'

'You shouldn't have climbed up all those stairs, Mother,' said Mrs Tranter. 'It's too much for you –'

'Well, where's the girl been, then?' asked Mrs Randall. 'Where've you been, girl?'

Kate said: 'To Sattin Shore.'

Mrs Randall was carrying her walking-stick – she had been using it on the stairs as a mountaineer uses an alpenstock. Now she banged the floor with it: 'No!' she exclaimed, and actually tottered on her feet as if struck a blow by her own anger. Mrs Tranter seized a chair, put it behind her mother, and helped her to sit down.

'Tell me!' Mrs Randall ordered.

Mrs Tranter said: 'Kate knew about the tombstone in the churchyard, Mother. She knew that Bob's name was on it, not Fred's. She knew when the tombstone went, but she didn't know why. So I've told her about the memorial masons and the new inscription for Fred's death. That's all I've told her.'

'All she needs to know,' replied Mrs Randall. To Kate she said: 'So your father is dead, after all. Forget him.'

'But, Granny –'

'I said, Forget him.'

Kate turned to her mother: 'Mum –'

'Katy . . .' said Mrs Tranter, in distress.

'No,' said Mrs Randall, interposing between them. 'She must just forget him.'

Kate's mother said nothing more.

'Help me down to my room again,' said Mrs Randall. She waited while her daughter switched off the electric heater and quickly tucked Kate up for the night. Kate and her mother did not speak together.

Then Mrs Tranter took Kate's bowl and spoon in one

hand, and with the other helped her mother up from her chair to begin the long descent of the stairs. 'Goodnight, Kate!' said Mrs Tranter; and that was all.

Someone else slipped out of the room with the other two: Syrup. He would never stay on Kate's bed at night while she slept – perhaps because she tossed and turned too much. He would even rather sleep on the bedroom floor; or better still, he would escape before the time for sleeping.

So Kate was left quite alone. The light was out; the door shut; she had been tucked up for the night, to go to sleep – and she could not sleep. She longed to sleep; but her mind kept puzzling away. How could you forget someone you had never known? Her grandmother had made it sound simple, straightforward, and – above all – necessary.

But surely, you had to know someone before you could forget them ...

Warmth and darkness and the tiredness of her body sent Kate drifting a little way into sleep.

She slept a little, then woke, feeling too hot, stifled. The whole room was stuffy after the electric fire; the darkness seemed suffocating. She could not breathe. She left her bed and went to the window. She drew back the curtains and opened the casement. The air was fresh, cold. The moonlight was cold, clear. She could see, in the distance, the church and the churchyard; the churchyard was speckled with the shadows cast by the tombstones. They stood, like a crowd of people, motionless, waiting.

Kate wondered if her father's tombstone – for it *was* his now, as well – was back in its place in the churchyard, from the masons' yard. Her mother and her grandmother had not told her that. Well, she could always go and see for herself.

She stood some time at the window, looking out, and taking deep breaths of the cool, clear air. Then she went back to bed. She left the curtains drawn back, and the window open.

This time she slept.

Chapter 10

EYES IN THE MIRROR

The next day, and the next after that, Kate stayed away from school, mostly in bed. She was glad to do so, and glad of the ordinariness of things at home. Ordinariness was restful.

The usual things happened; and even the unusual ones were quite ordinary.

She heard Lenny and Ran bickering downstairs.

She heard her mother furiously scolding Syrup. It turned out that he had caught a bird: he had smuggled the body indoors to eat in secret, and left the parts he did not fancy under the kitchen dresser. They were not found at once.

She heard the vicar arriving for a stately chat with old Mrs Randall, one of his church members. Kate peeped down at him from the stairs.

And she was well enough to be in the midst of the excitement of Mrs Tranter's discovery of the gas leak, that led to an emergency call (from a box) to the Gas Board and the arrival, after working hours, of three men and a van and several bags of tools. (The gas oven thermostat had also gone wrong, but the gasmen said that did not have anything to do with the leak and so the Gas Board would certainly not allow them to have anything to do with it, either. Mrs Tranter said she would like to knock the Gas Board's heads together. Lenny pestered in vain to have a go at the thermostat himself.)

Then Anna called. Of course, she wanted to know what Kate had been doing on the day she was supposed to have been with Anna, and hadn't been. Kate said she had just biked out into the country; and she said – with truth – that her mother had forbidden her to talk about it. Anna was not satisfied; but Kate went on hurriedly with the news of the gas leak, and of Syrup's dead bird.

'He managed so that nobody knew about it?' asked Anna.

'That's it!' Kate said gaily. 'Sly puss!'

'He's a cat, and cats have secrets,' said Anna. To make sure that Kate understood her reproach, she added: 'Having secrets from people is a nasty part of cat-character.'

Finally, Kate was well enough to go back to the routine of school. She reflected, then, that nothing much had really changed, after all. Just for a while, because of the disappearing tombstone and what followed its disappearance, she had thought otherwise; but she had been wrong. It was true indeed that her father had not died on the very day she had been born, but he had died all the same. He was dead, as she had always supposed.

On the way home from school, on her first day back, she called at the churchyard, but the tombstone was not yet back in its place. She called the next day, and the next: still no stone. The memorial masons were taking their time over the job. Gasmen came quickly in gas emergencies, but there were no emergencies in memorial masonry, to hurry the masons up.

Meanwhile, Kate became shy of visiting the churchyard. Workmen had appeared there to mend the vestry roof on the side of the church nearest to her corner. They piled slates and set up ladders. They took a break from their work to drink flasks of tea, and, while they drank, they surveyed the churchyard. Once, while they were watching her, Kate saw Syrup come round the corner of the church behind them. They did not see him; he saw them, of course – and their ladders. Syrup could never resist the lure of adventure. Kate watched him ascend the rungs of one of the ladders, paw after paw, and so reach the vestry roof. He prowled along it, and then climbed to the ridge and over, and disappeared from her view.

Kate waited for more than a week before her next visit to the churchyard: still no tombstone. By then the workmen had finished their job, and gone. She could visit the churchyard freely again. She called every day on her way back from school. On Saturdays she sometimes went twice.

In the churchyard, the grass was growing tall, lush and green. Crocuses were out; daffodils in bud. Soon it would be the Easter holidays, and Easter itself. But there was still no tombstone.

By now Kate found that she was beginning to dream again of tombstones that danced on fog-wrapped, satiny shores.

Yet again Kate went into the churchyard and towards the usual corner. From a distance, as usual, she could see where the tombstone should be standing.

As usual, she looked; and, this time, there it was.

She stopped at once, then advanced slowly, her eyes fixed upon the stone, as if it might try to escape from under her very gaze. She began to be able to read the capital letters incised upon it. At the top, the old, weather-worn inscription: JAMES TRANTER. Below that: ALFRED ROBERT TRANTER. Then, below again – she blinked –

her father's name, picked out in a black still shiny from its newness:

FREDERICK JAMES TRANTER

Still she came closer, still staring at the last inscription. Now she was close enough to read, below the capitals of her father's name, the smaller writing: the letters and numbers that told the date of her father's death.

She stared and stared.

Her mother had said that her father had died 'later – a little later'. Kate remembered her mother's odd hesitation on the phrase.

'A little later'? – Her father had died on New Year's Day of this very year!

She seemed to hear a voice from her dreams: her grandmother's voice crying, 'Look at this! Look – look!' Only this time Kate knew that she was remembering, not the dream, but an actuality: that afternoon in January when she had picked up, at the front door, a hand-delivered envelope addressed in violet ink, and propped it against her grandmother's teacup on her grandmother's little tray, and carried it in to her. That letter had brought the news of her father's death. She was sure of it now. She remembered her mother's saying, on the day of Sattin Shore: 'Word came to your grandmother – to both of us.' The word had been in the letter. She remembered, on the day of the letter, the dark look on her mother's face when she had come back from old Mrs Randall's room: she had read the letter: she knew. Kate remembered, and now she understood.

So recently, then, had Kate's father died: last New Year's Day. For all the years and months and weeks and days of her life up to this very last New Year's Day, Kate Tranter had had a living father, and she had not known it. And now he was dead.

She tried to think to herself: Nothing has really changed. It makes no difference when he died: he's dead now. But it did make a difference. She could so nearly have known him. Why, he could have decided to come and see his family this very Christmas! There would have been a ring at the front door, and Kate would have gone to answer it. She would have opened the door, and a stranger would have been standing on the doorstep, all hung about with parcels that were Christmas presents, and carrying a little Christmas tree. It was too dark in the doorway for her to see his face, but she could see his eyes looking at her, and he said: 'Katy – you must be Katy: I'm Fred Tranter come home. I'm your father.'

But, as if a heavy door had been slammed shut between them forever, he had died, this New Year's Day.

'Oh!' Katy cried aloud in the solitude of the churchyard, and she fell down on the grass in front of the tombstone and beat on the ground with her hands – not just in grief, but in a fury of grief, like a little child raging in bitterest disappointment.

She exhausted herself. She lay there, the front of her body cold and hard-pressed against the ground, her back in the warmth of sunshine. She lay still and quiet – so quiet that she could hear the slightest sounds of the churchyard.

A bird sang. Distant traffic. A light, quick sound that might be the click of the churchyard gate opening . . .

Suppose someone had clicked open the gate and come in, and saw her lying there, and stopped to pity her . . . Suppose her father walked into the churchyard and came and stood over her. He said: 'Poor Kate . . . Poor Katy . . .'

She heard no footstep on the gravel of the path; she heard no voice; yet she could feel that he was there. She said to him: 'I'm glad you've come.' She said: 'I've wanted you so much.' She said: 'Don't go. *Don't go.*'

Silence. A bird. Traffic.

Slowly she got up. She looked round her slowly, carefully. No one had come in through the gate. She was quite alone in the churchyard. Not even Syrup was there.

She walked home slowly, thinking of her father, absorbed in that thought. The thought filled her mind. The thought stayed with her when she fell asleep, and was in her dreaming; and she found it in her mind again when she woke up.

For three days and nights she thought almost all the time of her father, whom she had never thought of properly before at all. In her dreams and in her waking mind's eye she saw him, shadowy, with a shadowy face; but his eyes looked at her.

On the third day she came home from school early. Nobody at home, except for Granny in her room – and perhaps Syrup somewhere.

Syrup was not upstairs in her bedroom, so Kate left her door ajar. 'He may come later,' she said to herself.

'Later' – she wondered why the word troubled her. Then she remembered: 'later – a little later'.

She opened her window wide and leaned out on the sill, looking towards the churchyard. The sun still shone there, although her room had lost it. The sparrows were noisy above her, under the eaves: not a great din, but close, deafening. All the same, the sparrows did not bother her; but the window curtains did. A fitful breeze blew them to flap about her ears. They interrupted her thinking about her father and herself.

At last she drew back into the bedroom, but left the window still open behind her. The curtains still flapped.

She went to the chest of drawers, over which hung her mirror. She looked searchingly at the face reflected there. She stared at herself, remembering that once – once –

her grandmother had said sourly that she resembled her father. After all, she was her father's daughter.

She searched in the looking-glass for Fred Tranter in Kate Tranter. The longer she looked, the more the girl in the glass became a stranger to her.

She peered deeply into the mirror. Behind Kate Tranter's face lay the dimness of Kate Tranter's bedroom, all reversed and strange, as though strange things might begin to happen there.

In that background dimness a slight movement attracted her attention. The just-open door wavered as in a draught – it swung open a little wider – a very little wider. There was something else, too. Not Syrup, because Syrup would have appeared almost at ground level. This was much higher. At human eye level.

She looked, and her eyes met other eyes, through the shadowy gap of the door. Too dark to see the face properly; but she knew it was there, because the eyes looked at her.

Fright froze her.

Then, for a second, relief: this must be Ran.

Then terror – for this was not Ran. It was *not Ran*. The eyes of a stranger looked at her from over her shoulder, from the dim depths of the mirror.

Then a breeze blew, the window curtains flapped, the door swung gently back on to its door frame and clicked and was shut.

The eyes were gone.

Kate was clutching at the sides of the chest of drawers as though the house were rocking on its foundations and she might otherwise have been thrown to the floor.

Someone had been there: she could not – she *could not* have imagined it.

With an effort, she moved from the chest of drawers and sat down on the edge of the bed. She was dizzy. She had sweated too, coldly.

After a little while she was able to make herself get up and go to the door and open it. Nothing – nobody – outside.

She went downstairs to the hall. Just by the front door Syrup was crouching comfortably, dozing. He was waiting for someone to open the door, coming in or going out, so that he could slip out and away on business of his own; and he looked as if he had been waiting there patiently for some time.

So no one could have just gone out by the front door.

She checked that the back door was bolted on the inside, as usual, and that the ground floor windows were secured, as usual.

She determined to search the house, although by now she did not expect to find anybody. She picked Syrup up in her arms for comfort, if not for protection. He did not seem to mind being taken away from his planned exit. She began to search.

She poked into every cupboard and wardrobe, looked under every bed. In Ran's room she had to be careful: it was so orderly that she was sure he would have noticed the slightest disarrangement. His travelling alarm clock, which usually stood open at his bedside, was folded and lay on his work-table. She nearly opened it and moved it back to its proper place. Then she reflected that Ran himself must have folded it and put it there for some special reason: no one else would have dared to tamper with it. She left it alone, where it was.

She looked everywhere; no trace of any intruder.

She ended up in the hall again. She remembered that her grandmother saw many things through her partly open door.

She pushed the door a little wider. 'Granny?'

'Yes?'

'Did you see anyone in the hall just now?'

'That cat. And then you came from upstairs.'

'But no one went out by the front door?'

'No. Who should have done?'

'Nobody. And nobody came in, earlier?'

'You did.'

'But besides me?'

'Nobody. Who should have done?'

'I just wondered.'

Kate closed her grandmother's door to its previous position. She went upstairs again, still carrying Syrup.

At her mother's door she hesitated, then went quickly in. She knew exactly where to find what she wanted to look at. Under folded scarves and squares in a drawer lay an old photograph album and wedding photographs of twenty years ago: the wedding of Catharine Randall to Frederick Tranter. She studied the face of Frederick Tranter: she could not tell whether her face was like it; certainly Randall's was; Lenny's less so.

And the face she had seen – or rather, not seen – in the crack of her door?

She could not tell. She slid the photograph back into concealment, and left her mother's bedroom.

She went back to her own room, still with Syrup.

The window of her room was still open, the curtains still blowing, the sparrows noisy.

She closed her bedroom door behind her, then shut the window. She wondered whether the noisiness of the sparrows and the flapping of the curtains would have been enough to mask the sound of soft feet on the stairs. Or, on the other hand, had the draught through the window been enough to sway the door open a little and then sway it shut, without human agency at all?

She lay on her bed, holding Syrup to her, trying to think carefully of what had happened, or what she thought had happened – or what she had entirely imagined.

'But, Syrup, I didn't just imagine: I saw. I didn't imagine him. I didn't.'

If the intruder were neither a silly figment of her imagination nor a flesh-and-blood man whom she could have found in the house by searching it, then what was he?

The room had filled with shadows.

Kate brought her face close to Syrup's fur. She whispered into it what she dared not say aloud, openly: 'A ghost? Really a ghost?'

Chapter 11

KATE WITH ANNA

The day was sunny and cheerful, not a cloud in the sky.

Kate had climbed Gripe's Hill, not for the view, but for the airiness of the brisk little winds that blew round the top, and for the loneliness. There was no one in sight in any direction. She swivelled right round, slowly, to make sure of that, and ended up with her back to the distant view of the estuary.

There was no one within earshot.

She spoke aloud, with careful purpose: 'I'm Kate Tranter, who lives with her mother and her grandmother and her two brothers. I haven't any other family. There's no one else at all. My father died this year; but –' She hesitated, then went on determinedly: '– I'd never seen him, and he'd never seen me. So he wasn't important to me. He isn't important to me. Now he's dead, there's no point in thinking of him. I shan't think of him again. Ever.'

Something in the way she had spoken troubled her. Not clear enough? Not firm enough? Or perhaps too firm – mere bluff, bravado?

She turned to confront the distant gleam of estuary water. She shouted at it, but spacing her words out clearly, steadily: 'My father is dead and gone. That's the end of him.'

Then she began to run down the hill towards her bicycle at the bottom. The steepness of the hill made her go faster and faster, until soon she found herself bounding desperately, jarring herself at every downward leap – in danger of falling headlong – in danger of breaking an ankle – in danger of smashing herself to pieces –

She reached her bicycle, and managed to stop herself not far beyond it. She mounted and rode back towards Ipston, care cast from her and left behind.

Not entirely carefree, perhaps: Kate found that she disliked entering her own home alone, or being in it alone. The silent presence in her grandmother's room was no reassurance, no protection from shadowy fears. So she began regularly to seek to be with Anna; and Anna was delighted. They went home together after school, either to Anna's flat or to Kate's house. They did homework together. They had tea together in one place or the other. Afterwards they might go riding their bikes together, or go together to the swings in the Park, or swim together at the Public Baths. Sometimes they watched television together. Sometimes they just sat and talked, stroking the cat of whichever home they happened to be in.

Anna thought she was Kate's friend, just as Kate was hers. But Kate knew that Anna was also Kate's reassurance, her protection. She *wore* Anna, as some careful knight might have worn a suit of armour.

Mrs Tranter was surprised and pleased at the sudden increase in the friendship: no more solitary excursions and churchyard fancies for Kate; she would be like everyone else. Mr Johnson, Anna's father, was less pleased; but, as Anna spent as much time out of their flat with Kate as Kate spent in it with Anna, he could not grumble much. Besides, he foresaw a lightening of his worries when the holidays came: he, too, had his plans.

What Kate dreamed of at night, alone, she could not have told anyone, for she forgot her dreams as she woke from them. She wanted that.

In the daytime, if she were ever apart from Anna, she would not allow herself any thought of her father, or of any of the things that might lead her to think of him – the tombstone and the churchyard, Uncle Bob, Sattin Shore.

Only very occasionally did such a thought enter her mind, against her wishes, and by surprise only.

The first occasion was one market day. The Ipston market was not an important one, but even so, a good many people came in from the country round about to sell produce and to do their own shopping. Their cars and vans and lorries were allowed special parking in the side streets off the market place.

Kate and Anna were wandering among the market stalls, staring, fingering, exclaiming to each other. Besides the usual stalls of vegetables and fruit, there was cheap china, and junk of all kinds.

'Look, Cath,' said Anna, 'I like this dish for a cat.'

'Or a dog,' said Kate. She was not looking at the dish; she happened to be looking at a dog.

'Not a dish for a dog, with I LOVE LITTLE PUSSY written all round the edge!' said Anna. She thought this very funny; but Kate did not laugh.

Kate was staring at the dog she had noticed. It was a black-and-white terrier, and it was looking at her through the windscreen of a van. It sat alone on the front seat.

One black-and-white terrier is perhaps much like an-other, but this was a terrier sitting in a white van. Kate left Anna to go closer.

'Cath! Wait for me!'

Kate went to the side of the van, to see if there was anything written there. Yes: SATTIN HALL FRUITFARM LTD. She must have looked a few seconds too long for the peace of mind of the terrier. He began springing at the side window between them, barking and snarling, his body bobbing up and down in angry excitement.

Sattin ... It had somehow never occurred to Kate that, just as she could go to Sattin, so someone from Sattin could come to Ipston. The road between Ipston and Sattin ran in both directions. Perhaps the van came quite often ...

The little dog seemed as if it might shriek itself into a fit; and Anna had caught up with Kate: 'What is it, Cath?'

'Nothing,' said Kate, turning away from the van. She managed to push the thought of Sattin and Sattin Shore to the back of her mind, and then out of it altogether. 'Let's go somewhere else. This market is boring.'

The second occasion was in the Ipston Public Baths, to which Kate and Anna had gone early one Sunday morning. They were so early that they were the first people into the changing rooms; the first in the Baths. For a very short time they had the water entirely to them-selves.

Kate was swimming underwater, from the deep end to the shallow; up to breathe; then back again. No need to watch out for legs and arms that might appear in her watery way. Even Anna was still sitting on the side, just splashing with her feet.

Kate swam on, and thought this was the best under-water swimming she had ever done, and wished the water were always so empty of people. Even the sea at Sandby was not like this; and there waves often interrupted rudely . . .

She swam slowly to the far end, thinking of expanses of empty water, and began coming up, leisurely, for air, and thought of an empty sky overhead, instead of the roofing of the Public Baths – a sky empty except, perhaps, for a seagull or two, as there would always be on Sattin Shore . . .

She came up into the air of the Ipston Public Baths, with its smell of disinfected water; and already people were jumping or diving into the water and shouting and splashing and swimming. She was bewildered by her surroundings, because her mind was still filled – against her own wish – with the presence of another, more desolate place.

And she was beginning to think of her father . . .

'Anna!' she called, almost as if she were drowning; and Anna came bobbing towards her through the water, grinning. They were at the shallow end, so that both could stand easily, and Kate said: 'Let's not stay any longer!'

'But we've only just come!'

Kate said: 'I'm going, anyway'; and Anna, overborne, had to follow her.

In the changing rooms, Kate said: 'I don't like it here. I don't want to come again. There are other things we can do, and not come here.'

Anna said: 'Have it your own way. But I can't always be doing things with you, anyway.'

'What do you mean?'

'I was going to tell you. I'm to go away to my granny's when the holidays begin.'

'Go away!'

'My dad says he can't manage when I'm at home all

day, in the holidays, and he's at work. So I'm to go to my granny's.'

'Why can't your granny come and look after you in Ipston?'

'She can't. And my other granny –'

'Two grannies?'

'Everyone has two grannies.' Kate opened her mouth to contradict; and Anna corrected herself: 'Or has had them. My other granny is my mother's mother. My dad says she comes into our flat over his dead body.'

'Ooh!' said Kate, distracted for a moment. Then she came back to what mattered: 'So you'll really have to go?'

'The first Saturday. For all the holidays.' Anna's revenge on Kate for insisting on leaving the Baths was over. Now she said: 'I wish I weren't going, Cath!'

'So do I,' said Kate. 'Oh, so do I!'

When the first Saturday of the holidays came, Kate went to the coach station to see Anna off. Her father was there with her, gloomy as ever. He saw Anna into her seat on the coach; then he went away. Kate stayed until the coach left. She waved Anna good-bye.

Kate went home and wrote a letter to Anna, although there had not been time for anything really to have happened to tell her about. She posted the letter. Then it was time for Saturday dinner with her mother and grandmother. The two boys were both out.

Old Mrs Randall said: 'I suppose Ran's gone off somewhere with that girl of his.' Kate knew that by now her mother knew about Vicky; and her mother must have told her grandmother.

After the washing up, Kate played with Syrup in the back garden, up and down the rockery there. In spite of his age and his portliness, Syrup could still be tempted by the twitching of a piece of string. Kate tired before he did.

She felt aimless without Anna. Television on a Saturday afternoon was full of the things that she wasn't interested in; and she decided against going to the swings in the Park, alone. In the end, she stayed at home, reading, with Syrup beside her.

At the end of the afternoon, there was the sound of at least one boy returning. Kate went down to greet whoever it was. Randall and Lenny had just put their bicycles away in the garden shed. She was surprised: 'Did you go somewhere together?'

'Yes,' said Ran. He sounded in a good humour. Lenny did not speak.

'I saw Anna off from the coach station this morning,' said Kate. 'She's gone away for the holidays. For the whole of the holidays.'

'Bad luck!' said Ran. Again Kate was surprised, this time at his sympathy.

Lenny went past her and up to his room, still without speaking. She wondered if he were angry with her; but she could not remember anything she had done to offend him. Besides, Lenny was not usually silent in anger or irritation. No, this was something different.

'What's got into him?' she asked Randall.

'Oh, nothing!' said Randall; but she was pretty sure that he knew all about whatever it was. 'Tell you what, Katy,' said Randall, 'if you're at a loose end these holidays, I'll go on a long bike ride with you one weekend, shall I?'

She could not believe her ears. 'You'll take me on a bike ride?'

'Yes.'

She wanted to ask, 'Why?' but was afraid of making him withdraw his offer in a huff. So, instead, she asked: 'Where shall we go, Ran?'

'I'll think of somewhere.'

'Truly?'

'I've told you.'

'Oh, Ran!' She rushed at him and hugged him before she could stop herself. He did not seem to mind.

Chapter 12

SYRUP

The prospect of the bicycle trip with Ran buoyed up Kate's spirits at the beginning of these Anna-less holidays. Yet when the time came for Randall to say he was ready to go, Kate absolutely would not.

Syrup had disappeared.

One evening, in the middle of that week, he had not turned up for his supper and to settle indoors for the night. This was most unusual; but Mrs Tranter pointed out that even the most home-loving of cats likes a night out occasionally. Syrup would be mewing to be let in the next morning.

But Syrup did not come back the next morning. Nor that afternoon. Nor that evening.

Abruptly they all became anxious – and Kate became frightened as well. She had already called him everywhere in the house and the back garden. Now she looked for him in all the places where he might have been shut by accident: the shed in the garden and the tool-chest in it, the cupboards and even the wardrobes in the house …

That day and the next she went on Syrup's rounds in the neighbourhood, as far as she knew them. Neighbours were concerned to hear Kate's story, but they had not seen Ginger (as they called him) for some time.

She went into the churchyard and scanned it, and walked round the church, eyeing all the windows. But the church windows were not even made to open, she discovered. Only the vestry had a little modern casement, which could be opened from the inside. Kate remembered Syrup's mounting to the vestry roof, when the workmen had left their ladder there: perhaps he was particularly attracted to the vestry, and had found the casement window even a little open, and had entered that way, and then later the window had been shut. So he might be shut in the vestry.

She went round to the main door of the church, but it was locked. That only made Kate more determined, even hopeful.

Mrs Tranter was at work at the confectionery, where Kate was usually shy of going. But now, without hesitation, she went there, asked for her mother, and told her of her suspicion of the vestry. Mrs Tranter took ten minutes off to go with Kate to the vicarage for the church key.

On the way Mrs Tranter gave Kate an odd, sidelong look: 'You say you saw Syrup on the vestry roof not long ago? You were in the churchyard, then?'

'Yes, I was.' Kate did not care about churchyard secrets any more. All she wanted was to hold Syrup in her arms.

The vicar himself took Kate to the vestry, while Mrs Tranter hurried back to her work.

The vestry was just a small, shabby room built on to the main structure of the church, with one window. There was a large cupboard, fastened but not locked. The vicar opened it. The cupboard was full, mostly with hanging surplices.

Kate poked about in the cupboard. 'Syrup?' she whispered; but he was not there.

'You know,' said the vicar, detaining Kate with his eye, 'it's interesting to remember that the ancient Egyptians believed that cats went to a special heaven. When they died.'

'Why?' said Kate. 'I mean, why is it interesting?'

'Something for you to think about,' said the vicar, and began to sort prayer-books in a preoccupied way. Kate left him.

She walked down the nave of the church towards the main door, which the vicar had left standing open. She could see bright sunlight outside. Inside, the church was a large, cold, stony emptiness round her; not at all the place where Syrup would choose to be. But then, had she not come to the conclusion that that was exactly where he must be – somewhere he did not want to be? Shut up. Imprisoned. Without even water, perhaps. And for how long now?

What had the vicar been getting at with his talk of heaven for ancient Egyptian cats that had died?

Died?

She halted in the middle of the nave and called at the top of her voice: 'Syrup! Syrup!'

The vicar appeared in the doorway to the vestry. 'My dear child!' he called softly, perhaps in protest against her violation of the stillness, perhaps to begin some kind of condolence.

Kate fled.

Instead of going home, she went to the police station. A young policeman listened to what she had to say, and made notes. Then, looking down at what he had just written, he said: 'You know, cats aren't like dogs . . .'

Kate was taken aback. Looking up sharply and seeing her expression, the man plainly became embarrassed, fiddled with his pen, cleared his throat –

But an older policeman, who had been listening, leaned

across the station counter to say to Kate: 'Dogs stray and often they're brought in to us. Cats aren't. And if a cat's run over and killed –'

Killed?

'– well, a dead cat's not brought in to us either. It's left, or just found and buried. You see?'

Kate could not bear the kind gaze of the two policemen. Again she ran.

Still she did not go home. She roamed the back streets round about, calling 'Syrup!' until people came to their windows to look at her. One sharp-faced boy shouted to ask if she were advertising a bargain offer of groceries. She gave him a look that silenced him.

'Syrup! Syrup!' she called incessantly.

An old man tapped on a window to attract her attention, then opened it to speak to her: 'Are you calling someone?'

'Our cat. He's called Syrup because he's that colour. A kind of golden yellow. Have you seen a cat like that?'

'I think it may be the same we call Sunshine. He drops in on us sometimes for chicken scraps.'

'Our cat – you can't mistake him: the tip of his tail is bent.'

'That's our Sunshine!' cried the old man. 'Our Sunshine to a T!'

Kate loved the old man – she could have hugged him through the half-open window, she was so happy. 'We thought we'd really lost him,' she explained. 'Greedy old Syrup, to stay so long with you!'

'But he's not with us,' said the old man. 'We haven't seen him since about Tuesday. We've been wondering why.'

Kate hated the old man; she drew away from him. 'You say you don't know where he is?'

'No. But there's another house he calls at in our street.' He told her the number. 'Try there.'

She tried at the other house. The woman who answered the door told her that the ginger cat with the funny tail, whom they had nicknamed Sunny Jim, had not been seen since the beginning of the week.

At last Kate was going home – by now there was nowhere else to go to. As she entered the front door, her mother hurried to meet her: 'Any luck?'

Kate shook her head. She was trying not to cry; but the tears began to trickle, and then stream from her eyes. Her mother put her arms about her, began to talk useless comfort to her.

The door of old Mrs Randall's room opened wide. She stood in the doorway, to address them both: 'Depend upon it, that cat's dead. The girl had better make up her mind to it.'

'Mother!' said Mrs Tranter.

'And, after all, it was only a cat.'

Kate lifted her face from her mother's shoulder: 'It was *Syrup*,' she said. Then, realizing that she herself had spoken of him in the past, as dead, she uttered a wail, broke from her mother and ran upstairs.

She threw herself on to her bed and drew the coverlet over her head and cried, not loudly, but as though she would cry forever.

Chapter 13

THIRST AT MIDNIGHT

No one disturbed Kate in her bedroom, until her mother crept in to persuade her to come down to some tea.

'I'm not hungry. I'm not thirsty.' Kate refused to come.

Later, Randall came up to try to coax her downstairs; but she would not go. He left her, and after a while she cried herself to sleep, them woke to remember that she had lost Syrup, and cried again, and dozed.

As she dozed, she was aware that the household was going, one by one, to bed. Her mother paid her a last visit, probably to get her at least to undress and get properly into bed. Kate pretended to be sleeping deeply, and again she was left. This time she fell really asleep.

She woke later to the quietness of a sleeping house. She lay awake, thinking with piercing grief of Syrup. At the same time she found that she was thinking of herself: she felt hungry (she had had very little midday dinner, and no tea or supper at all); she was also thirsty – very thirsty. She must drink something. Yes, she must drink.

She decided to get up and go downstairs to the kitchen, where she could drink a mug of water or milk. She left her bed, opened her bedroom door, and stepped out on to the little landing that she shared with Lenny. She had moved quietly, and now she stopped moving: the house was absolutely still and silent round her. The remembrance of the eyes seen in the doorway came back to her, but now she could dismiss that from her mind easily.

Stillness . . .

Silence . . .

Then, faint but unmistakable – no illusion, no hallucination – she heard it: a cat's *miaow*.

Then silence again. She had heard the voice, yet she could not believe that she had heard what she had heard. She stood without moving, held her breath, listened, waited –

Again, faintly, *miaow*.

'Syrup?' she whispered. Then called softly again: 'Syrup?' Then waited.

In answer, *miaow*.

Where was he? She opened the door of Lenny's room and called into the darkness: 'Syrup? Syrup?' In his bed, Lenny stirred.

Kate could not be sure where the answers had come from, but at least not from Lenny's room. She left Lenny's door open, without caring, and began moving downstairs: 'Syrup?'

The mewing she heard in reply now surely sounded more distant. She halted on the stairs: 'Syrup?'

This time there was no answer. She called a little more loudly: 'Syrup?' Still no answer. Again she called; again no answer. Then she panicked: she called Syrup's name not once but over and over again, in quickest succession, without lowering her voice or ever waiting to hear whether he answered her.

Her cries woke the house. Mrs Tranter was the first to come running up the stairs to where Kate stood. 'Kate! Kate!' She seized hold of Kate, grasped her and then shook her. Was the child sleepwalking, or having a nightmare, or what?

Next Randall was coming: 'What is it? Why's she screaming?'

Even Lenny came from his bedroom, staggering from sleep: 'What? Who?'

Kate glared round at them all. 'I heard him! I heard Syrup! Then he stopped. But I did hear him – *I heard him!*'

'Kate!' said Mrs Tranter, who had stopped shaking Kate and was now just holding her. 'Kate, listen to me!'

'No, I won't! Because I heard him – I heard him – I heard him –'

'Then let us hear him, Kate! Be quiet, Kate! Everyone be quiet! Quiet, and see if we can hear anything.'

Instantly Kate was silent. They all stood in silence. Then a sound came, but from below. Old Mrs Randall's voice came up the stairs to them: 'What's wrong? Catharine! Catharine!'

'Nothing wrong, Mother. I'll be with you in a moment.' Then at once to Kate: 'Quick, Kate! While the house is quiet, call him.'

Kate controlled herself, and then called softly but carry-ingly: 'Syrup!'

Silence. Then the faintest answering mew – but every-one heard it.

'Where is he?' breathed Mrs Tranter. 'Where?'

Lenny said: 'He's above. He must be in the roof.'

'In the loft?' cried Mrs Tranter. 'He can't be! How could he have got up there? It's impossible!'

Randall said: 'I think Lenny's right, though. I'll get the loft-pole.'

'No, I will!' cried Kate – and she was already rushing down to her mother's room. She brought the pole back with her, held under her arm like a lance at the charge; her family parted before her, making way for her to use the pole. But she was shaken by such anxiety and eagerness that the trembling of her hands did not allow her to hold the pole steadily upright. It wavered – nearly fell – 'Ran, help me! Oh, help me quickly!'

He put his hands firmly over hers and together they gripped the loft-pole and raised it up – up – until its end touched the catch of the trapdoor. Then, together, they pressed –

The catch gave: the trapdoor opened, swinging downwards.

A square of shadowy darkness appeared above them.

A dusting of roof-dirt floated down upon them.

A pair of ghost-eyes looked greenly out at them.

'It's Syrup!' cried Kate. 'Oh, dearest, dearest Syrup! It's you! You're alive after all! Oh, Syrup – Syrup – Syrup –'

Ran was pulling the loft-ladder down. At the movement and the grindings and clankings that went with it, the eyes disappeared. They reappeared as Kate began to mount the ladder. At the top, she reached out with her arms, and Syrup let her take him into them and carry him down with her again.

'He's so thin – so thin!' said Kate, as she caressed him. 'And he's so dirty, too! Poor, poor Syrup!'

'There's an awful stench up there,' said Lenny, sniffing. He had mounted a few steps of the ladder.

'Well, there would be, wouldn't there?' said Randall. 'A cat shut in for days. No earth. No cat litter.'

'But how did he ever get shut up there?' asked Mrs Tranter. 'How?'

Kate cared only for Syrup. She carried him down to the kitchen, passing her grandmother standing in the hall, and ignoring her questions – not noticing even that they were being put. She carried Syrup into the kitchen, and mixed water and milk and warmed it to blood-heat in a saucepan. She poured a little into a saucer and let Syrup drink it. He lapped weakly, and yet with a terrible eagerness. Then she made him wait a little, so that he should not drink more than was good for him all at once. While she waited, she touched him tenderly and lovingly, making sure that he was not injured in any way. But all that Syrup was suffering from was hunger and thirst – thirst above all – and the weakness and tiredness that come from that condition.

When he had been allowed to drink, at careful intervals, as much as he needed, Syrup cleaned himself just a little, then dozed off on Kate's lap. The saucepan was still half full of his milk and water, and now Kate remembered her own thirst. She gave herself a mugful of Syrup's drink. Although she was so thirsty, she did not drink off the mugful at once, but sipped it at intervals, as Syrup had done; and she thought of Syrup all the time, and let her free hand rest gently upon him.

By now Mrs Tranter had soothed her mother with an explanation of what had happened, and had seen her back to bed. Then she had come into the kitchen and made tea for them all – for all except Kate, dreamily sitting and sipping her milk and water.

Everyone was relieved at Syrup's return; everyone was glad. Yet, as she poured the tea, Mrs Tranter frowned. 'I just don't see how Syrup ever got up there in the first place.'

'Up the loft-ladder,' murmured Kate, without bothering to think much. 'He can't resist ladders, you know.'

'But who's been giving him the chance? – Who's been using the loft-ladder recently?' asked Mrs Tranter. 'Kate?'

'No – oh, no!' If Kate had used the loft-ladder, or even seen it in use just before Syrup's disappearance, she would have remembered – as she had remembered the ladder to the vestry roof.

'Lenny? Your friend, Brian, must have been the last

person – at least, I thought he was the last person – to go up, months ago, when he put the toboggan away.'

'I haven't been up there, Mum. Honestly. Nor has Brian, except that once.'

'Well, then – Ran?'

'No. Why should I want to sneak up into the roof, anyway?'

That was a good point: what reason would anyone have for going secretly up into the roof, leaving the ladder down just long enough for Syrup to mount it, unobserved? And *secretly*? How could anyone get into the loft secretly, when the mere pulling down of the loft-ladder made such a din?

But Mrs Tranter turned again to Lenny: 'Are you sure you haven't been up, quite recently, to check on that toboggan for some reason?'

'No, I swear.'

Mrs Tranter continued to stare at Lenny.

Kate had at last finished her milk and water; and she had become more aware of what was being said in the kitchen. Looking at her mother's face, she could read its expression: Mrs Tranter did not believe in Lenny's denial.

Kate felt sorry for Lenny: trouble lay ahead for him.

Chapter 14

NAN

Kate was happier than – it seemed to her – she could ever have been before. Syrup had been given up for dead; and he was alive. He had been lost; and he was found.

In her happiness she hardly noticed what other events were taking place around her. She knew that there was a terrible cat-mess in the loft, and that an even more terrible row was going on about it. As a kind of thanksgiving for Syrup restored, Kate had offered to clear the mess up herself. Fiercely her mother had said, No! Lenny was responsible for the cat's getting up into the loft: Lenny must clear the mess.

But Lenny continued to deny that it was he who had used the loft-ladder for any purpose at all at the time of Syrup's disappearance. And his mother continued to disbelieve him.

In the end, Mrs Tranter insisted absolutely that Lenny should clean the loft. He did so in sullen fury.

Nor did the matter end there. Mrs Tranter had punished Lenny both for what she was sure was his responsibility and for his denial of that responsibility. When the punishment was over, the denial still remained; and that denial angered Mrs Tranter more than anything else. She tried again and again to manoeuvre Lenny into a confession.

Lenny was embittered by her accusations, wearied almost to tears by her pleadings and pressures; but he maintained his innocence.

Meanwhile, Syrup was recovering his health and his beauty. Anna, back at the end of the holidays, heard the story of his nearly fatal adventure: she assured Kate that he already looked as well and as handsome as ever. Kate listened gratefully, her gaze always on Syrup.

Now Anna wanted to change the subject of conversation. She was excited at the prospect – but guiltily so: 'Cathy!'

'Yes?' Kate was feeling for Syrup's ribs under his fur.

'Listen!'

'I am listening ...'

'I'm leaving Ipston!'

'But you've only just got back!'

'I mean, leaving for good.' Kate had stopped caressing Syrup; she stared at Anna. Anna went on: 'My dad wants us to move from Ipston altogether, to be nearer my granny – the granny I've been staying with. My granny could be a help in all kinds of ways, he says. And my granny's willing.'

'But, Anna, you're my friend!'

Anna said: 'There'll be other people to be friends with. And you've got Syrup. And you've got your family, and there are more people in your family than there are in mine. You do nice things alone with your family.'

Kate knew at once what Anna was thinking of: the cycle ride that she, Kate, would be doing with Randall some day soon. The trip should have taken place while Anna was away, but Syrup's disappearance had put it from every mind. Now Anna was back; and when

Kate went off with Randall, she would be leaving Anna behind.

'I don't want to do things without you,' Kate said to Anna; and that was true. 'I don't want to go biking off alone with Ran, just the two of us' – and that was untrue: she wanted two contradictory things at the same time.

'But you will go off with Ran without me,' said Anna; 'that's just what I mean.' There could be no gainsaying her.

When the time came, Randall arranged everything for the cycling expedition. If Kate had been noticing more carefully, she might have wondered that he checked her bicycle over, as if they were going a long way, yet took no provisions, as though they would need none; they did not take even any drinking-water with them. He was vague when Mrs Tranter asked where they were off to. She did not press her question: Kate would be safe with Randall.

They left Ipston on one of the first Saturday mornings of true summer. The route at first took them past Gripe's Hill. They cycled on, Kate on the inside, Randall setting the pace, but not too fast for her. Their way took them through villages and by country roads. Everywhere trees were coming into full leaf, and the grass verges were starred with wild flowers.

Kate was happy – too happy to bother her head with wonderings and questionings. But she began to notice the names of the villages they came to, and to recognize them.

'But, Ran –'

'Come on, Katy, we want to be there by dinnertime.'

'To be where, though? Where, Ran?'

Then he told her: 'Sattin.'

She was alarmed. 'But Mum told me – and Granny said –'

'Forget them,' said Randall. 'Forget them both, just this once. This is a secret between you and me and Lenny.'

'And Lenny?'

'I brought Lenny on this same trip – oh! weeks ago!'

Yes, Kate remembered their return from some long cycle ride on the day she had said good-bye to Anna at the coach station. She remembered Lenny's odd quietness then.

Kate now accepted that this expedition was Ran's to lead just as he wished. She did not ask what they would do when they reached Sattin – go down to the shore, perhaps.

But they did not do that. They stopped outside the old school. A holiday family were in it for the weekend; they stared at Randall and Kate as if they were extraordinary-looking foreigners.

Randall lowered his voice: 'This was the school, and we lived there.' He nodded to the brick-built cottage next door. Then he looked at the cottage on the other side of the school, and said: 'I should think you could get a drink of water there, by asking.'

'I'm not thirsty yet,' said Kate.

'You will be. You'd better get your drink now. Go round to the back door and ask.'

'Come with me, then.'

'No, I've got something to do to the chain on my bike. You go. You'll be all right.'

Kate wanted to refuse, but she would not cross Randall on a day such as this; and she knew he knew it.

She left her bicycle with Randall and went in through the front gate and up the front path. The front door faced her, and she could see why she must not knock there, or ring the bell. The doorstep was moss-grown, even in the middle of its tread, and a spider's web bound door to doorframe: the front door was not in use.

Kate followed the path from the front of the house to the side and so to the back door. She knocked, and at once the door was opened, almost as though the person inside had been waiting for just such a knock. The person opening the door was the same little old woman whom Kate had seen weeding in the front garden on her previous visit to Sattin. They recognized each other. Kate expected no special welcome, but she was surprised by the expression on the old woman's face: displeasure.

Kate would have liked just to go away, but it seemed too late for that. She said nervously: 'Please, could you let me have a drink of water?'

'It's not very convenient, really – but, of course, yes!' The old woman managed to smile at Kate; but she said: 'I hope you'll drink it quickly. I shan't ask you in, for I'm expecting company, you know. It would be awkward.'

Kate said nothing.

The old woman brought a tumbler of cold water, and Kate began to drink it. After all, she was quite thirsty.

The old woman was fidgeting for her to finish and go. 'I remember you,' she said. 'You came before. You're Anna Johnson.'

Kate stared, then remembered her cover-story. 'Oh, yes . . .'

She finished her water, and the old woman was quick to take the empty tumbler from her. She was just about to shut the door on Kate, when Randall came round the corner of the cottage from the front.

'Well?' he said, apparently to both of them.

To Kate's amazement, the old woman addressed Randall directly, and as if she knew him well: 'This is

Anna Johnson. She's only called for a drink of water. She's going now.'

Randall, astounded, cried: 'But, Nan –!'

Then Kate was bewildered: 'Ran, why do you call her that?'

The little old woman was the most perplexed of them all: 'Where's my Kate?' she asked.

Then they began to explain. Kate explained to Randall about Anna Johnson: the little old woman listened closely and – to Kate's wonderment – began to cry. Then it was Randall's turn to explain to Kate: 'I called her Nan because she's our grandmother.'

'But our granny's at home in Ipston!' cried Kate.

Weeping tears of joy, the little old woman was clinging to Kate: 'Kate – Kate! Oh, my dear! I'm your other grand-mother! In Ipston, there's your granny Randall; but I'm your granny Tranter! I'm your daddy's mother. I'm your Nan that's always longed and longed to see you and Randall and Lenny, and to kiss you.' And she kissed Kate.

Kate said: 'If you're our Nan, why've you never come to see us?'

'Oh, my dear!' The little woman seemed to shrink with fear before Kate's eyes. 'I dared not have done such a thing, my dear! I daren't – I daren't! There'd been such hard words spoken – such quarrelling! Oh dear, dear me ...

Randall put an arm round the distressed old woman. At the same time he explained to Kate: 'After Uncle Bob was drowned – on the day you were born, that is – we all moved to Ipston, and our other grandmother would never let us have anything to do with Sattin again.'

Now Kate understood things she had not understood before; and she saw that Randall now knew things that he certainly had not known when he first spoke to her of an Uncle Bob and a Sattin Shore. They were things he must have learnt from this little old woman who was their other grandmother, their Nan, as Randall called her.

She understood why Lenny had been so strangely quiet, as if overwhelmed, after his return from Sattin with Ran: from what she, Kate, was feeling, here and now, she could guess how he must have felt then.

Ran had brought Lenny to Sattin to meet the grandmother Lenny had known in infancy and long forgotten. But what had brought Ran to Sattin in the first place? Or who had summoned him? Not, surely, such a timid little old woman as this new Nan of theirs ...

And why *now*, and not at any other time, earlier or later? Why *now*, when a visit had been impossible before, so it seemed? For years and years, impossible; and *now*, suddenly –

But, 'Come in! come in!' the old woman was imploring them. 'I'm all ready for you both – I've been waiting for you!'

This was no time for questions. Perhaps later ...

Kate allowed herself, with Randall, to be drawn indoors, into the front room – the best room – of the cottage. In the middle of it, taking up most of the space, stood a large table spread with a white cloth and bearing a feast for them: there were Scotch eggs and Cornish pasties and pigs-in-blankets and fresh lettuce and radishes and pickled onions and pickled beetroot and pickled walnuts and cheese and rhubarb crumble and egg custard and junket and jellies of three colours. And there was a great jug of home-made lemonade.

No one could have failed to look at the table first of all; but, after that, Kate looked round the rest of the room. Unlike any room in her other grandmother's house in Ipston, this room was full of photographs. Some of the people in them she recognized, chiefly because she had seen them in the album her mother kept hidden in her drawer.

She recognized the wedding photograph of Catharine Randall and Frederick Tranter; but this was another version of it. At Fred Tranter's shoulder stood a third figure – a man whose face seemed distantly familiar to Kate.

'Who is it?' she asked.

'The best man at their wedding, my dear: Arnold West. Arnie still farms here – Sattin Hall Fruitfarm.'

('So that's it,' thought Kate.)

'He was a friend to my two boys, and he's good to me still. He does me many kindnesses.' Nanny Tranter gave an odd, sad little laugh, and said: 'He's like another son to me.' Then she sighed; and then she said, 'But you must sit down and eat: you're hungry.'

Old Mrs Tranter refused to sit down herself. She fussed round them, asking them questions about themselves, often without waiting properly for the answers, because she was always pressing them to eat this or try that or 'just a little more'. Whatever she asked them about, she never mentioned their mother or their other grandmother.

Kate told her about Syrup and his being lost and then found ('That's good!'), and about her friend, Anna Johnson (they laughed again about the muddle of the name), and about Anna's going away from Ipston ('That's bad!'). Kate told about tobogganing on Gripe's Hill and Lenny's sprained ankle; but she never mentioned the letter that had come even before the snow with the news of Frederick Tranter's death. She never mentioned the churchyard and the vanishing tombstone.

As Kate talked, she felt Randall's eyes upon her, as if he feared what she might say next. But she knew about being tactful and discreet, didn't she? She was asking no questions.

Randall ate fast and stopped eating long before Kate; and soon – too soon, Kate thought – he began to talk of setting off home again.

Chapter 15

KATE GOES BACK

Old Mrs Tranter was looking out a photograph of her son, Frederick, for Kate to take home with her. 'He'd like you to have it,' she said to Kate. Then she corrected herself: 'He would have liked you to have it.' Once before Kate had noticed this grandmother speaking of her dead son as if he still lived: strange to be old and to remember so much of the past that the past crept in upon the present and met and mingled with it.

Old Mrs Tranter wrote on the back of the photograph, '*For my granddaughter, Kate*'. Kate stared at the inscription, in rheumaticky-looking handwriting of bright violet ink. She remembered where she had seen that ink before, on an envelope, hand-delivered but not by any postman. She remembered footsteps briskly receding from the front door and then the sound of a car being driven away – only the car must have been a van – a white van. That hand-delivery had been one of Arnold West's son-like kindnesses to Nanny Tranter.

Some questions answered themselves, Kate thought, if you waited long enough.

Now, as though she had decided that the party was

over, Mrs Tranter had begun to carry the used dishes through into the scullery. She was going to start washing up at once, without waiting for her guests to leave. But Kate still wandered round the room, looking at more photographs; Ran stayed with her. Several times Kate noticed his glancing uneasily at the clock on the mantelpiece.

Kate had found another wedding photograph, this time of the bride and bridegroom surrounded by all the wedding-guests. She looked at them, one by one. She could recognize Granny Randall and Nanny Tranter, sitting as far as possible away from each other. She could not even guess at anyone else, except for bride, bridegroom, and best man.

Kate asked: 'Where's our Uncle Bob?'

'Not there, my dear,' said old Mrs Tranter. She had come back into the room to fetch the last of the dirty dishes from the table. 'Abroad at the time, he was.'

Kate knew about weddings from conversations at school. She said: 'If he'd been in England, he might have been best man instead of Mr West.'

Old Mrs Tranter turned to look at her, and laughed slyly. 'Best man? Bridegroom, more likely!' Then she was frightened at having said too much, and turned abruptly away.

But, 'What do you mean?' asked Kate.

Over her shoulder, as if these things were of no consequence, old Mrs Tranter said: 'Your mother fancied Bob at one time. He could have had her. But he didn't want her – then. She married your father.'

'We might have been *his* children,' said Kate wonderingly.

'We'd just have been ourselves, whoever our father was,' said Randall. Kate could feel that he disapproved of this conversation, and now he decided to cut it short: 'We ought to go, Nanny.'

'Don't go!' she cried.

'We must – you know we must.' He glanced at the clock, so that she saw his glance.

Mrs Tranter said quickly: 'Go! You're right, Randall! Go at once!'

'Shall I come again?' asked Kate.

Her grandmother kissed her repeatedly. 'Of course! Of course! But we may have to wait a little while. A step at a time ... Randall knows ...'

'Yes, arrangements ...' said Randall.

Kate looked from one to the other: they seemed to be talking to each other over her head about some complicated plan of which this visit was only a part.

'But I just want to come and see Nan again!' said Kate.

'So you shall, my dear – so you shall! All in good time!'

Randall and old Mrs Tranter hurried Kate out of the house and down the front path to the bicycles. The visitors mounted. Old Mrs Tranter waved them good-bye. Even as they began pedalling off, she had turned her back upon them to trot indoors again.

They had ridden only a few yards when Kate braked suddenly. 'I've left my photo!'

'What photo?'

'The one Nan gave me; and she wrote on the back. I left it on her table. I remember now.'

'It'll keep till next time.'

'No, I want it.' As she spoke, she was off her bicycle and leaning it against the fence.

'There isn't time! You can't go back!' Randall lunged with a hand to try to catch her, to stop her. She dodged him.

'I'll only be a minute, Ran. I won't talk to Nan, I promise.'

'Don't go back!' cried Randall. But she had gone already.

Up the path and round the side of the house to the back door, which had been left open. In she went, into the empty front room. There was her photograph on the table. She picked it up. She would take it away without her grandmother even knowing that she had been. The old woman was in the scullery, washing up with enough of a splash and a clatter to cover any sound that Kate made.

Kate peeped into the scullery for one more look at this amazing discovery, another grandmother, her new Nan.

Old Mrs Tranter stood at the sink with her back to the scullery door. Just over the sink was the window that looked right down the cottage garden to a little gate in the fence at the bottom. The old woman had explained to Kate that this gate had been put in by Arnold West, so that she could more easily get to his house if she needed him. His orchards began where her garden ended.

There was a click as the gate at the bottom of the garden opened. Kate peered to see who was coming; so did the washer-up at the sink.

First through the gate came a black-and-white terrier, just ahead of its master. Then Arnold West himself. Behind him, and obscured by him, another figure. Kate could see, by the way the first man opened the gate and held it, that he was making way for the second man to pass him into the garden. At the same time, the dog was called to heel.

All this had been observed, too, by the washer-up. She ceased work to open the window over the sink and call joyfully down to the end of the garden: 'Come along! Come in! They've gone!'

They've gone? The words sounded in Kate's head in a way she did not like. She felt like a spy who has learnt more than is necessary – perhaps more than is good for him. Quickly she turned to leave by the way she had come.

As she reached the back door, she could already hear foot-steps on the path from the back garden. Out through the back door she went, turning at once on to the path to-wards the front; but – almost against her will – she looked back over her shoulder as she went. The two men and the dog had come into view: the dog and its owner were now in the rear; in front was the other man, a stranger.

He was a stranger, with eyes that had immediately seen Kate, eyes that fastened themselves upon her – upon her eyes. For two – perhaps three – seconds they stared at each other, eyes recognizing eyes.

The man opened his mouth as though he were going to speak; Kate thought she saw a name already on his lips: 'Katy . . .'

Kate turned and fled.

Out in the road, Randall was waiting for her with the two bicycles. 'All right?'

She managed to say: 'Yes. I got the photo. Nanny never saw me. She was in the scullery. She was washing up.'

'So it was all right, then?'

'Yes.'

They cycled off again, homeward bound. Several times, as they rode, Randall tried to start a conversation. Kate hardly answered.

They passed through village after village, and now here, on the side of the road, stood a telephone box, apparently no different from any other telephone box, and yet Kate recognized it: here she had stopped when she had been coming home alone.

As they approached the box, the telephone inside began to ring. They both heard it; and Randall laughed and said, 'How idiotic!'

'Why idiotic?' Kate had stopped pedalling, and Ran now slowed down with her.

'It can't be anyone! No one rings a telephone box!'

They were almost up to the box; the bell was still ringing.

Kate braked, stopped. She said: 'It *is* someone. It must be. It might be someone with a message for me.'

Randall said angrily: 'You're out of your mind, Kate! It can't be for you. Nobody could know you'd be passing just at this instant, and – oh! the thing's ridiculous!'

Randall had often been angry with Kate; but Kate had never been angry back – or never like this. She raged: 'How do you know – how do you *know?* There might be someone somewhere who saw us setting off from Sattin and knew the way we'd go home and the speed we were going and calculated we'd be here just when we are here!'

The bell still rang, rang, rang ...

'Kate, you're making it all up. Be reasonable, Kate.'

'Oh, you know everything!' shouted Kate. 'It's for me, and it must be important. I'm going to answer it, be-cause –'

The bell still rang, rang, rang ...

'– *who knows who it might be?*' And Kate had left her bicycle, almost flinging it from her, and rushed to the box to be there before the telephone stopped ringing.

Randall had to accept this lunacy. He got off his bicycle to pick up Kate's, and then stood, holding both bicycles, waiting.

He watched Kate, in the telephone box, pick up the receiver with the care of someone not used to telephoning often. He could hear nothing, but through the glass sides of the box he could see that Kate was listening, then speaking, then listening again. At last, she put down the receiver and was coming out of the box.

'There was someone?' Randall asked, disquieted.

'Oh, yes!' She could hardly control laughter, while she gasped out her words: 'A man. He had a car. It had broken down. He thought he was telephoning a garage.

He thought I was a garage.' She was almost shrieking with laughter now. 'He was so angry when he found out it was just me! It was just an angry man on the telephone!' She was sobbing with laughter now – so Randall thought at first; and then he saw that the sobs were with tears. She wept and wept. She bent over the saddle of her bicycle, as if in an agony of stomach ache, and wept and wept and wept.

Randall put an arm round her shoulder and held her tightly. He said: 'Kate, when you went back into the house for your photo, did you perhaps – was there perhaps someone –?'

'I saw someone,' whispered Kate. 'I'd seen him before. Someone a bit like you, Ran, but quite different, and much, much older. Old enough to be your father ...'

'Yes,' said Ran. 'He is my father – our father, Kate. He's Fred Tranter, alive, and come back.'

For what seemed a long time, Kate said nothing; then she said: 'Ran, you must tell me, now, without waiting. Tell me the truth. So that I know the truth.'

'I'll tell you all I know, Kate. Now.'

And so he did, beginning at the beginning.

Chapter 16

THE TALE OF A DEAD MAN

At the beginning of Randall's tale lay a dead man. He lay in the moonlight on Sattin Shore, his naked body wet with the water of the estuary. He lay face downwards, drowned.

'Drowned – I know!' Kate said impatiently. 'Uncle Bob was drowned. I know all about that – I know it all!'

'Do you?' said Randall. 'Are you sure, Kate?'

'Yes, of course. Don't tell me what once happened. Tell me again about *now*: it's our dad, Fred Tranter, in Nan's cottage now, isn't it?'

'Yes.'

'So he didn't die! And when I thought I saw someone looking at me, in our house –' She told Randall of the wind blowing the bedroom curtains, the door moving open a little: the eyes that looked at hers in the mirror.

'Yes,' said Randall. 'He did come to the house. He came to leave a message for me, without anyone else knowing, and – well, perhaps he wanted to see the inside of the house again. It's our home, and it was the house that he knew long ago from his courting days. It sounds odd, but he'd always kept the key to the house, that he'd been given then.'

'He left a message for you?' asked Kate.

'He wrote to me to come to Nan's cottage in Sattin to meet him. It was the first I ever knew of his being alive. He left the note where I'd be sure to find it, shut up in my alarm clock.'

Kate remembered the travelling alarm clock, folded shut and left on the top of the chest of drawers, where it should not have been.

'So he let himself in by the front door,' she said, and paused on that, for something worried her. But she left that little worry, and went on: 'How did he get out?'

'By the same way, I suppose.'

'Oh, no!' She told him of Syrup asleep against the front door, playing sentry without knowing it.

'Then he must have got out some other way.'

'No. I looked: the back door and all the windows were still fastened on the inside.'

'Then he hid himself somewhere inside the house, and slipped out later.'

'No. I looked everywhere – everywhere!'

'Oh, Kate!' cried Randall, exasperated in his old manner. 'You make such a big mystery of little things! What does it matter!'

'I suppose it doesn't.' She was able to put the little worry and what Ran had called the big mystery to the back of her mind. She said: 'Ran, I want to do something – now!'

'What?'

'Go back to Nan's cottage. See our dad. Talk to him.' She wanted to speak to him, and to hear his voice in answer. She would hear his voice saying: 'Kate ...' She would touch him, and be touched by him. 'Come on, Ran! We're going back!'

She had gripped her bicycle with the purpose of turning it to go back the way they had come. But Randall did not move. 'No. We can't go back, just like that. It's not as simple as that.'

'But it's our dad . . .'

'Kate, you didn't ask any of the questions I thought you'd ask.'

'Questions?'

'Why he disappeared for more than ten years . . . Why our granny and our mum made believe to us that he was dead, when they knew he wasn't . . . Why he came back secretly, having got our Nan to write to Granny in Ipston to say that he had died abroad . . .'

'Well, why all those things?' asked Kate. She fastened upon the last question: 'Why did he get Nan to send the letter saying he was dead?'

'So that he could come back secretly, without anyone expecting him. He thought it might be necessary for his safety.'

'For his safety?' Kate stared.

Randall took Kate's bicycle from her and laid it down on the grass verge. He laid his own beside it. He made Kate sit down on the grass outside the telephone box and near enough to lean back against it. He sat down beside her.

'His safety?' repeated Kate, and shivered.

Randall began his tale again with the drowned man in the moonlight on Sattin Shore, and a second man with him.

'They'd gone down to the shore just past midnight, the two of them,' said Randall: 'Fred Tranter and his brother, Bob.' (He spoke of his father and his uncle as if they were no relation to him, only shadowy characters in a tale he had to tell.) 'They were going to have a moonlight swim. When they got to the shore, Fred Tranter changed his mind – he said the water was too cold. Bob Tranter went in, but the cold of the water caught him as he swam – he wasn't used to it, after being abroad in hot climates. He got cramp. He was drowning, out in the middle of the estuary. Fred Tranter went in after him, and managed to bring him ashore. He was unconscious by then; he'd stopped breathing. Fred Tranter had life-saved him in the water, and now he life-saved him on land. He got his breath going again. He didn't leave him – he was positive about this afterwards – until he was sure he was breathing properly. Then he left him to fetch help from the village – help to carry him back. He knew he couldn't manage any more by himself. He was exhausted – dead beat, very nearly.'

Randall paused in his narrative. Kate had been seeing the shore in the moonlight. Now she saw the long track back from the shore to the village. She saw a man running along it in the moonlight, nearly exhausted, sometimes staggering, stumbling, gasping, but always running on for help – help – help –

'He got help all right, in the end,' said Randall. 'He went first to the fruitfarm, of course, because he came to it first; but Arnold West wasn't there. He was away in Sattin Wood, watching owls. He's a bird-watcher, you know.

'So Fred Tranter went on. He didn't go to his mother's cottage, or to his own schoolhouse, because it was a strong man he needed, or several men. He had only a little further to go to the village, and there he managed to rouse people, and in the end there were three or four men and they took a van and drove as fast as they could back to the shore. But, by the time they found Bob Tranter, it was too late.'

'Too late?'

'Fred Tranter had forgotten the tide coming up the estuary from the sea. The tide had come up. Not very much; not very deep. Only about six inches under Bob

Tranter, but the water came over his mouth and nostrils as he lay. He had drowned in six inches of water. This time they couldn't bring him back to life, although they tried and tried. He was dead.'

'Oh!' cried Kate, seeing the expanse of the estuary waters, silvery-sweet in the moonlight, and the narrowness of the strip of shore between water's edge and shrub-grown bank. 'Oh! He forgot the tide! How could he have forgotten? How could he?'

Randall said: 'At first, afterwards, he said he didn't forget. He said he'd taken care to drag his brother well above the tide-line. He said that Bob Tranter must have come to and crawled, and crawled in the wrong direction, towards the incoming tide, and then collapsed again within its reach. But that really wasn't likely – just wasn't possible. So the doctor said. And, at the inquest, the coroner said that it was understandable but sad that, in the fearfulness of the emergency, Mr Frederick Tranter had forgotten to allow for the rising of the tide. Otherwise, the coroner said, Mr Tranter had behaved with exemplary courage and resourcefulness.'

'How do you know all this?' asked Kate.

'I went to the office where they keep the records of inquests. By the end of this inquest, Fred Tranter had stopped saying he was sure he remembered dragging his brother above the tide-line; he just shut up about it.'

Kate thought hard; she remembered detective stories she had read. 'Surely, if Uncle Bob had crawled, there would have been crawl-marks on the shore. Something. *Something.*'

'Nothing. Not after half a dozen men had tramped all over the place in the dark to find the drowned man.'

'But it was moonlight – you said.'

'Not by then. It had clouded over; it was pitch dark. They had to fumble about on the shore for their man;

and, when they found him, they had to try to bring him back to life, working in turns on it, and finally giving up, and lifting the body and carrying it away. So there were no clear signs left on the shore; just a jumble of tracks.'

'Go on,' said Kate.

'They brought the body back to Nan's cottage – Bob Tranter had been staying with his mother. In the schoolhouse, our mum was still up, waiting for our dad to come in. Her mother – I mean, Granny – was with her, on a visit from Ipston. When word came from the cottage, our mum went over at once, but Granny stayed where she was because of the two children asleep, Lenny and me.

'When our mum saw the body, she was in such a state that, there and then, she began having the baby – you. She was rushed off to hospital, and in the end she had the baby, but she was terribly ill. The hospital thought she might die. By the time she was well enough to come out of hospital, the inquest was over, and our dad had disappeared. Granny fetched Mum from hospital, with you, and took her straight to her own house in Ipston. Lenny and I were already there. We've all lived there ever since.'

A long silence. Then Kate asked the question that she had to ask: 'Why did our dad go off like that? Why did he disappear for ten years?'

Randall looked at her steadily. 'There were things that weren't mentioned at the inquest.'

'What things?'

He still did not answer her directly, but said: 'Sattin was a bigger village in those days. More people – more gossip. People whispered that Fred Tranter had always wanted Bob Tranter dead ...'

Kate sat motionless; even her breathing seemed not to stir her. 'Go on.'

'People were saying that Fred Tranter made sure Bob Tranter died that night. That he deliberately left him below the tide-line ...'

Again he waited for Kate to speak. At last she said, 'You mean, people believed that he'd murdered his brother?'

'Everyone knew the brothers didn't get on. They quarrelled often. There was that business of Bob Tranter's nearly marrying the woman who became Fred Tranter's wife.'

'Our mum ...'

'People said that Bob Tranter had come home because of her. He gave as his reason that he meant to go into farm-partnership with Arnold West; but Arnold West was the only person who really believed that. Fred Tranter didn't.'

Kate cried out: 'But that night, the two of them were going to have a moonlight bathe together! Together, like friends! You said so!'

'After they'd patched up the worst quarrel yet. People knew that. Nobody spoke up against Fred Tranter at the inquest; but, afterwards, they wouldn't forget. He was afraid of their whisperings, and he was afraid of what they'd begin to say out loud if he stayed around after the inquest. He was afraid of what our mum might think.'

'She couldn't think he was a murderer?'

'Ah, but it wasn't just her. There was Granny. Our mum was her only child, and she'd always wanted to keep her to herself. Granny was jealous of Fred Tranter – she was jealous of all the Tranters. That's what Nanny says.'

'Nanny – Granny – Nanny – Granny!' cried Kate: the names rang like little angry, chattering bells in her mind. 'What's it to do with them *now*? I just want to see my dad again!' She began to cry.

'And so you shall, Katy! That's why our dad's come home again. He wants to have his family again – all of us. He'll try every way he possibly can to have us all again.'

Kate wiped her eyes. She said sadly: 'Resourcefulness, you mean. But not much courage, really – not for ten years.'

'What?' said Ran. He did not recognize his own quotation from the coroner at the inquest.

'It doesn't matter,' said Kate. She got up and lifted her bicycle into position. 'So we go home now?'

'If there's nothing more you want to ask me, Kate, about what I've told you.'

She said: 'Such a muddle! Such a mess! Everybody hating everybody else … Everybody afraid … Everybody pretending what isn't true …'

Randall sighed heavily. He said: 'If there's any part of it all that you think I could explain, then ask me. Any little thing …'

Kate's mind flitted back to the day of Fred Tranter's secret visit to the house in Ipston: his coming, his going. The little worry and the mystery came to the forefront of her mind again. But she knew that Randall could help with neither.

'Yes?' said Ran.

'Nothing,' said Kate.

They mounted their bicycles and rode homeward.

Chapter 17

TWO PILLOWS

They rode back to Ipston together; but, on the last lap
of the journey, Randall was glancing down uneasily at
his watch – he had arranged to meet Vicky at her
house, and he was late.

So he said to Kate; and Kate thought: *We're late because
we sat down outside a telephone box to talk about murder*
... All that now seemed so strange, so weird, so unlikely.
Now, she could hardly believe what she had been told
then – now, when they were cycling along together in
such an ordinary way, through ordinary familiar streets,
almost within sight of their own home.

At the end of their street, Randall said good-bye to Kate:
'And remember, Kate, don't say anything at all to Mum
– not anything. Or even to Lenny: he knows about Nan
now, but not about our dad. We must wait for the right
time to tell about our dad. The right time, remember;
and it's not yet.'

'When will it be, then?' asked Kate; but Randall just
said that depended.

Perhaps it partly depended on their father's courage,
Kate thought.

Kate arrived home alone. She took her bicycle in through the back garden, in order to put it, as usual, into the house by the back door.

In the garden, surprise halted her. Here was Brian, Lenny's friend; but no sign of Lenny himself. Brian sat on the lower slopes of the rockery, facing the back door, hands clasped and hanging floppily between his knees, waiting. At some distance, also facing the back door, also waiting, sat Syrup.

Syrup's waiting gave Kate the clue: he waited outside in this way when something was going on indoors that he disliked – a dog-visitor, the gasmen, or just the Tranter children making an uproar for some reason. He waited outside until disturbances were over.

What Brian told her showed her supposition to be correct. Lenny had brought Brian home with him to tea; but, as the two of them walked into the house, Mrs Tranter had pounced on Lenny. She made some excuse – so Brian said; then almost at once began to re-accuse Lenny of using the loft-ladder at the time of Syrup's disappearance. The accusation was exactly the old one, but it had been made so many times that both sides were now near breaking point. Almost immediately Lenny was shouting at his mother in exasperation; his mother was shouting back.

Brian had decided to go out and wait in the garden. There he was joined by Syrup.

All this had happened not long ago. The rowing of voices from inside had gone on until just now, Brian said; then they had dwindled suddenly, and then stopped altogether. It was odd, their stopping altogether.

Kate listened carefully. The silence seemed perfect. She led the way back into the house, pushing her bicycle ahead of her.

At the sound of Kate's entry, Mrs Tranter appeared

in the kitchen doorway. She looked pale, tired; her hair was dishevelled. 'So there you are!' she said rapidly: 'Lenny has admitted that he was the one who used the loft-ladder, when Syrup disappeared.'

'What?' Kate heard her mother, but could not believe what she heard. She had always taken for granted that Lenny was telling the truth about the loft-ladder, chiefly because he usually did tell the truth – and why should he lie about it, anyway?

In bewilderment she said again: 'What?'

'I don't know why I have to repeat everything to everybody,' said Mrs Tranter crossly. She raised her voice: 'Lenny did use the loft-ladder. He confessed it, of his own free will, here in this kitchen!'

Her voice carried through the quietness of the house. Perhaps Lenny had been standing on the top landing, or perhaps he had been sitting on the stairs, listening: at any rate, his mother's words reached him and brought him rattling down the stairs in a human avalanche of fury. 'No, no, no!' he was shouting.

And even as he was descending, the door of old Mrs Randall's room, from standing merely ajar, began to open wider ...

Words rushed from Lenny to batter his listeners: 'I didn't confess of my own free will! You made me – you nagged and nagged and nagged me! When I told the truth, you wouldn't believe me. You only believe me when I tell a lie – when I *confess*! But now I take that confession back. I confess nothing, because I've nothing to confess. I didn't do it, I say! I DIDN'T DO IT!'

Lenny stopped for want of breath, and his mother, also breathless from his assault, stood mute. Kate and Brian just behind her, were mere spectators.

Meanwhile, the door of old Mrs Randall's room had opened wide: in the opening stood old Mrs Randall herself.

She said: 'This has got to stop. You must leave the boy alone, Catharine. He didn't do it; I did. I used that loft-ladder, when I had the house to myself one morning.'

They all looked at her – stared at her. She did not bother to repeat her words, but waited, looking composedly at them all.

Lenny was the first to believe her. 'Why didn't you say that before, long ago? Why did you let Mum go on and on at me? You should have said – you should have! Why didn't you?'

His grandmother made no reply.

Mrs Tranter said, 'Mother, you can't possibly have used that loft-ladder. You mean to say you went upstairs, got the loft-pole, managed to open the trapdoor and get the ladder down, and climbed into the loft? You couldn't do it!'

'I could, and I did,' said Mrs Randall. She made as if to close her door and so end the conversation.

Her daughter moved forward to detain her. 'But why on earth should you want to do such a thing? You might have fallen – you might have killed yourself! Why did you do it? Why? Why?'

Old Mrs Randall was clearly most reluctant to give any explanations. 'I wanted something of mine that had been stored away in the roof against my wish, without my knowledge at the time.'

'But, Mother, one of us would have got it for you, if you wanted something. What was it, anyway?'

'My private suitcase, the blue one.'

Mrs Tranter thought for a moment. 'But that's got two pillows in it – two pillows, that's all! I remember thinking it might as well go up into the loft.'

'My two pillows, of pure down. I wanted to have them. I wanted them quickly.'

'But – but –' Mrs Tranter was bewildered. 'Why ever

couldn't you ask one of us to get the suitcase? There's nothing secret about a suitcase with two pillows in it. Or why not ask me for another pillow, from the ones I keep ready?'

'I wanted my own pillows of pure down,' said Mrs Randall.

'But you haven't been using extra pillows, anyway – not even one extra pillow!'

'I am quite certain,' said Mrs Randall, 'that I shall need at least one of my pillows in the very near future. So, please, Catharine, let me mind my own business, and you mind yours.' She withdrew into her room, closing the door completely this time. Mrs Tranter and Lenny were left facing each other.

Mrs Tranter looked at Lenny; Lenny looked down at his toes. Mrs Tranter said, almost piteously: 'I'm sorry, Lenny. These last few days – and before that – oh, I apologize ... I do apologize ...'

Lenny lifted his head, and he looked at his mother; and she stretched out a hand towards him. He ignored it. 'You and Granny, between you!' he said. He turned and went back upstairs. They heard his footsteps on the last of the stairs, on the top landing, going into his room. Then, faintly, the sound of his bedroom door shutting.

Kate and Brian had seen and heard everything; so had Syrup – from outside. He judged, quite correctly, that all raised voices and hasty movements were now over. He sidled in past Brian, past Kate, past Mrs Tranter, and so into the kitchen.

'Well,' said Brian, 'I think I'll go home.'

Mrs Tranter looked at him dazedly. 'Why are you here, anyway?' She looked at Kate: 'And Kate ...'

But she did not wait to hear what either of them might have to say. She turned and went back into the kitchen, closing the door behind her.

'I think I'll go,' Brian repeated; but he lingered. He said: 'Kate, one of your tyres is flattish. I think you may have a slow puncture.'

His manner was odd; Kate looked at him wonderingly.

He said: 'I can't see the tyre properly indoors. Wheel the bike back into the garden.'

She did so. When the bicycle was outside the back door, he took it from her and wheeled it to the far end of the little garden, squeezing his way past the rockery to get there. Kate followed him.

Brian turned to face her, and Kate knew from his expression that he was going to ask questions. But he could not ask his questions without first giving away his own – his very own – private information; and he was reluctant to do that.

He hesitated, then said: 'Do you think your granny may be planning to run away from home?'

Kate burst out laughing.

He was annoyed: 'All right. She wouldn't exactly be *running*, perhaps; but she's certainly keeping a lot of ready money by her, for some reason. Why?'

Kate said: 'What makes you think she's a lot of money by her?'

'I know she has.'

'How do you know?'

There was no way out of it for Brian: 'I'll tell you how. You remember when I put the toboggan away in your loft? Well, I happened to be poking round there a bit –'

'Fancy that!' said Kate; but Brian ignored her.

'Among all the other stuff, there were several suitcases. One was a blue suitcase, with a label that said, TWO DOWN PILLOWS. I opened the blue suitcase with a key from one of the other cases: I wanted to have a look at the pillows – to find out how a down pillow is different from an ordinary pillow. So I handled the pillows in the blue suitcase – both of them.'

'Go on.'

'One of the pillows felt like an ordinary pillow, only much, much softer – sort of slippery-soft, when you squashed it. The other pillow wasn't soft at all: it felt all wrong for any pillow. So I opened it up, just a little, to find out what it was stuffed with. I felt right inside. The second pillow wasn't stuffed with down feathers or feathers of any kind: it was stuffed with paper.'

'*Paper?*'

'Paper money – banknotes. Lots and lots of money, all in notes.'

Kate goggled at him. 'Are you sure?'

'Of course I'm sure! I nearly came downstairs and told Lenny, there and then; but I didn't.' (Brian liked getting knowledge; he also liked keeping it to himself.) 'Thinking things over, I realized the money was someone's private affair. I thought then it was your mum's. Now I know the money's your gran's. Well, people do sometimes hide cash in their houses – especially old people. You read about it in the newspaper. But *now* – why should she suddenly want to have all that money downstairs with her *now* – without anyone's knowing, too? Why should she want it so badly that she goes up into the loft all by herself – and then lets Lenny take the blame? Why?'

'I don't know,' said Kate. 'Why ask me? Ask Lenny or my mum – or my gran.'

'None of them will want to talk about that blue suitcase for a long, long time,' said Brian. Then, 'Kate, do you remember the time, just before the snow and the tobogganing, when we were all having fish for tea, and your gran shouted out for your mum to come quickly?'

'No,' lied Kate.

'It was all so odd: that's why I remember. You don't

think there's some connection between your gran's shouting out then and her getting all this money down now?'

'No,' said Kate.

'How do you know there's no connection?'

Kate wanted to say that her grandmother had called out because of a hand-delivered letter and its news, and that this news could have nothing to do with a pillow stuffed with money. But she must tell nothing. She simply said: 'Why should there be any connection?'

'Because things often do connect. They fit together. In the end, everything has to make sense.'

'This doesn't,' Kate said firmly.

Brian was dissatisfied; but they had to leave the subject there.

He prepared to go. Then he came back. 'But that tyre really needs pumping, Kate. Unless it's a slow puncture. Watch out.'

But Kate was not going to bother now about possible slow punctures. She was glad to see Brian go. She put the bicycle back in its place indoors, and then started upstairs. She felt tired with the experiences of the long day; she felt lonely – and yet too tired for human company. She paused on the first steps of the staircase. She thought.

She turned and went down again to the kitchen. She opened the door a little and looked in. Her mother sat with her elbows propped on the kitchen table, her chin resting on her clenched fists. She was looking fixedly at the wall opposite. She never turned her head when the door opened, or when Kate softly called to Syrup.

Syrup had not been enjoying the kitchen, as he could usually rely upon doing. There was nothing for him to eat, nor were any eatables being cooked. Moreover, although there was stillness in the kitchen, there was not the tranquillity he had expected. He lifted his head when Kate called, interested in what alternative she might offer. She tempted him with soft words, and he let himself be tempted. He walked unhurriedly to the door and through the opening she made for him, and curved himself round her legs. She shut the door again upon her mother.

Kate picked Syrup up and carried him upstairs to her bedroom. She saw that Lenny's bedroom door was shut; and no sound came from behind it. She carried Syrup into her own room and shut the door behind them.

So the four people in the house were shut into their four rooms, each person quite alone – except for Kate. Kate had Syrup; she was the lucky one.

Chapter 18

STRAWBERRY-PICKING

The pillowcase stuffed with paper money bobbed on the surface of Kate's mind for only a very short time; then sank to the bottom. What really mattered was Sattin, the new grandmother there, and, above all, their father's return.

Kate would have liked to talk with Lenny about Sattin, but she feared to let slip the secret of their father. Ran had said 'Wait'; but for how long? Clearly for as long as Fred Tranter hesitated to declare himself alive and in their midst – at least, only those few miles away, in Sattin.

Ran had said 'Wait'; but already here was the middle of June. Kate had always loved June: sun and strawberries and the nearing of her birthday in July. This year, however, her birthday seemed a small thing; and there was no June sun. Every day, curtains of rain closed round the houses of Ipston. Old Mrs Randall's house was no exception.

Shut indoors by the rain, Kate and Anna talked – mostly in Kate's house, because Anna's father had begun to say he couldn't do with visitors, as they were moving before the end of summer. Kate talked with constraint, because her mind was filled with what she must not speak of; but Anna chattered on about the new little house in the new street in the new town that she and her father were going to, and the new school she would be attending in September.

In the end, tiring, Anna noticed Kate's own silence, and she reproached her: 'There's something secret again you won't tell me!'

'No – oh, no!'

'You should trust friends; friends can keep secrets.'

'I do trust you!' In a panic, Kate dredged her mind for some unimportant secret to tell Anna, and remembered the pillowcase of money. She told Anna – and regretted the confidence almost as soon as she had made it.

For Anna seized upon the subject, enlarging its possibilities. Suppose old Mrs Randall really had fallen from the loft-ladder and been killed? Then, said Anna, no one – absolutely no one (except for Brian, who didn't seem to count, Kate noticed) – would have known about the money in the pillow. So the pillow would be sent off to a jumble sale. ('But my mum would never send a good pillow to a jumble sale!') Or, better still, said Anna, the pillow was burnt with other rubbish on a bonfire. ('But my mum wouldn't burn a pillow on a bonfire – ever!') After that bonfire, charred banknotes floated over the neighbourhood. There was even a thousand-pound note, Anna said, every part of it burnt black except for the figure of one thousand, which was plain to be seen. Voice hushed, gaze fixed, Anna brooded over the ruin. Almost, she gloated. Yet there was no ill will towards her friend, Kate.

That dreadful bonfire decided Kate. She must tell her mother about the unimportant pillow. It was only a

question of waiting for the right moment, and then telling.
But, again, waiting . . .

Meanwhile, the strawberry season had begun, sun or
no sun. It was the worst of seasons. The punnets of strawberries on Ipston market were few, and poor. The topmost
strawberries usually looked well enough; but underneath
were fruits soft to collapsing merely under the weight
of those above them. And the price!

The Tranter children had always gone strawberry-
picking, usually on the same fruitfarm just outside Ipston.
They picked for their mother to make jam and, of course,
they ate as they picked.

This season, day after day, the rain fell and fruit-picking
was almost impossible. On what was perhaps the last
Saturday of the season, there was a break in the weather.
The sun came out with surprising heat; the moisture-
laden air appeared to steam. Not good weather for picking;
but the strawberries would wait no longer.

There were no less than seven pickers in the Tranter
party. Kate had brought Anna, Lenny had brought Brian,
Ran brought Vicky, and Vicky brought her little brother.
This was the first time that Ran had brought Vicky on
such a family expedition; and this was the first time that
Kate had thought of Vicky as possibly having any family
besides parents. Vicky's little brother had never picked
strawberries before.

The party, each person with a basket or bag, scattered
over the strawberry field, among the other pickers already
there. Kate and Anna chose to go to the remotest rows,
where only a stout woman in a pinafore was at work.

Because of the rains the strawberry leafage was lush
– high-growing and richly green. From this cover rose
one or two gorged blackbirds, as Kate and Anna approached. They flew unhurriedly off to some other strawberry patch without pickers.

The earth-ways between the rows were slimed into mud; the leaves were mud-spattered. Kate moved the strawberry leaves to and fro, and the strawberries gleamed up pinkly to her from the gloom beneath. Most of them were more pink than red, and those that had ripened red had ripened and rotted at the same time. Kate's finger and thumb squashed unpleasantly into the berries as she tried to hold fast to pick. Or she would turn what seemed a perfect fruit to twist it from its stem, only to find the underside frothy with grey mould.

The taste of the strawberries was thin, sunless. Still, they would make jam; they would have to.

After a while, Kate found that Vicky's little brother had joined them. He had had enough of picking strawberries and of eating them. He turned his attention now to the pickers.

He gave a little belch and said to Kate: 'Your mum's picked lots more than you have.'

'My mum?' Then Kate realized he meant the stout, pinafored woman still picking not far away. 'That's not my mum!'

'Who is she, then?'

'How should I know?'

'Where is your mum?'

'Not here. She's at home. She's waiting to turn these strawberries into jam.'

'Where's your dad?' Then: 'Why do you look like that?'

'Like what?'

'Like you are looking.'

'Oh, go away!' said Kate.

He went away just as far as to Anna. Kate heard him ask: 'Where's her dad then?'

'He's dead,' said Anna.

'Why didn't she say, then?' asked the little boy, aggrieved. 'I know about dead people. Why didn't she say? Why?'

'Go and ask silly questions somewhere else,' said Anna.

He rambled off among the rows and ended up distantly beside Brian. 'They'll ask each other questions – they'll enjoy that,' said Kate, watching them in conversation.

After an hour or more, the Tranter party had had enough of picking. They assembled again at the weighing-in shed. An old man sat there, reading to pass the time; he read very slowly, finger to word after word of his thick book. He stopped only when he had strawberry business to do. His job was to see that all bags and baskets were weighed empty, before picking began. Then, later, he weighed them full, made his calculations on a piece of paper, which he also used as a book-mark, and took the money for the weight of fruit.

When his turn came to pay, Randall remarked: 'The strawberries are much dearer than last year.'

'And worse,' said the old man. 'Rotting in the fields. Not moth nor rust, but corruption all the same. You've reaped corruption, that's what you've done.' He held out his hand for the money.

Randall paid – from money his mother had given him – for all the Tranter strawberries. He also paid for Anna's, for she had agreed to put hers with theirs: her father did not make jam, and she had eaten too many on the strawberry field to want to eat any more at home.

Strawberries went into bicycle baskets and carriers; and the party was ready to start back.

Kate was pumping up a tyre of her bicycle. Brian, looking across to her, said: 'Isn't that the slow puncture?'

'It's *very* slow,' said Kate.

'You ought to mend it.'

'Yes,' said Kate, who hated mending punctures because she was so bad at it. 'I will mend it. I'm only waiting ...'

The old strawberry man had been listening. He did not raise his eyes from his columns of close black print, but said, as if reading aloud: 'If I wait, the grave is mine house.'

'Silly!' Anna whispered to Kate; but Kate said: 'I'll mend it this afternoon.' Anna offered to come and help her; Kate refused.

As Kate and Anna rode off after the others, Kate was thinking: 'Anyway, I hate waiting. I hate it.'

At home, Mrs Tranter had an early Saturday dinner ready for them all. She said she wanted the dinner eaten and the washing up done and the kitchen ready for jam-making as soon as possible. 'Your granny and I will be at it all afternoon.'

After the meal and the clearing up, Randall and Lenny both went out; they would not be back until teatime at the earliest. Old Mrs Randall settled in her usual chair at the kitchen table, to hull strawberries. Mrs Tranter was getting everything else ready: the preserving pan with a dab of butter on the bottom inside; the sugar; the jamjars heating gently in the oven ...

'And what about you, Kate?' her mother asked. 'Anna coming round as usual?'

'No,' said Kate, regretting now that she had an afternoon of puncture-mending by herself, instead of an afternoon with Anna.

'So you're going to hers instead?'

She so hated puncture-mending ... She found herself saying, 'Yes, I think I'll go round to hers,' and immediately afterwards thinking that she must not once again put off this puncture business. She must do it first. She must do it now, at once.

But it was too heavily hot to start that kind of work

at once. Instead, she climbed the stairs to her room. All the windows and all the inner doors of the house stood open to let the air move, if it would. Even the trapdoor to the loft hung down, to let the heat of the house escape into the roof. Kate looked up into the darkness of the square above, where she had once seen Syrup's eyes looking down – oh, blessed sight!

She entered her bedroom, and there was Syrup himself on the bed, welcoming her with a stretch of his limbs and the beginning of a purr. She sat down beside him, and then lay down, fondling him. She decided to read just one chapter of her book, in Syrup's company; then the puncture.

She lay down with her head on the pillow, and Syrup in the small of her back. She began reading, but holding the book became inconvenient. She let it slip twice, and then let it lie.

The room was stuffy, even with window and door open. She closed her eyes.

She closed her eyes: she must have slept, or nearly slept. She seemed to hear her mother call her name from below, two or three times. She could not be bothered to answer.

If she had been listening carefully, Kate would have distinguished something particular in the way her mother called her name. There was a query in it, that meant: 'Kate, are you still there?'

But Kate did not answer, and the silence in the house said to Mrs Tranter: 'Yes, Kate has gone, as the other two have gone. You and your mother have the house to yourselves.'

Mrs Tranter, standing in the hall, listened to the silence. Then she turned, but not back to the kitchen, where Mrs Randall was keeping watch over the preserving pan on the cooker: Mrs Tranter went purposefully into her mother's empty bedroom. She rummaged under the bed. She came out again and crossed the hall to the kitchen, carrying a blue suitcase.

If only Kate had realized, there had never been any need to tell her mother about the money-pillow. Not for a moment had Mrs Tranter really believed in her mother's need suddenly to have extra pillows to hand. She had taken the first opportunity of being alone in the downstairs bedroom to find the suitcase, examine its contents, and – like Brian before her – she now knew the secret. What she still did not know was the reason for the hoarding of so much cash and for her mother's fetching it so secretly by that extraordinary climb into the loft.

Mrs Tranter seldom tackled her mother on any doubtful subject; but today she was going to. Entering the kitchen, she said: 'I want to have something out with you, Mother. We shan't be disturbed; we're alone in the house. It's about your money . . .'

Old Mrs Randall had seen the suitcase, but she said nothing. With her long wooden spoon she was stirring the jam in the preserving pan; it was beginning to come up to its rolling boil.

Mrs Tranter had put the suitcase down in the doorway, and she prepared to open it. 'Don't bother,' said her mother. 'Since we both know what's inside, evidently.'

'But, Mother, why – why –'

'I'm glad you ask me for an explanation now, Catharine,' said Mrs Randall, always stirring with her long spoon. 'It's better that I tell you everything, now we're alone, as you say. From the beginning . . .'

Upstairs, on her bed, Kate stirred, hardly asleep anyway. From below mounted the delicious smell of fresh strawberry jam; it reached her nostrils. She opened her eyes. The smell was of no interest to Syrup, who dozed on, but to Kate it was alluring. She must not miss the scraping of the pan.

She yawned, swung her legs to the floor, got up and began going slowly downstairs to the kitchen.

Chapter 19

A STATUE ON THE STAIRS

Kate descended the stairs slowly because she was still very sleepy, and she met the smell of strawberry jam ascending. It came more and more strongly, until she could almost taste its sweetness in her mouth.

Now she could just see the kitchen doorway, and see partly inside it. She saw a rectangular blue shape in the doorway and recognized it as her grandmother's blue suitcase.

Another slow step or two down the stairs, and she could hear the murmur of a voice talking – her grandmother talking. Yes, and she could just hear the words: her grandmother was describing an unexpected visit she had once had.

Kate paused on the stairs, to listen.

Kate had missed the beginning of this story; but she gathered that the visitor had been unexpected and very unwelcome, too.

Who? wondered Kate, and leant against the wall by the staircase to yawn a strawberry-flavoured yawn.

He – her grandmother called the visitor only 'he' and 'him' – had wanted to go upstairs.

An odd thing, thought Kate; *odd as things in dreams are odd* ... And she yawned again.

Old Mrs Randall had not wanted her visitor to go up, but she could not stop him. Fortunately, there was nobody else in the house at the time, except for – Kate was suddenly wide awake as she heard her own name – except for Kate.

Then she realized – then she knew!

No unimportant reminiscence, this! This was the story of Fred Tranter's coming here on the day when she had seen his ghost-eyes through her bedroom door.

So her grandmother had known – she had always known!

Kate's mind was working hard while her grandmother was still talking. 'He would go upstairs,' old Mrs Randall was saying, '– why, I don't know ...'

But I do, thought Kate: *to leave his note for Randall, in the alarm clock.*

'Unless,' said her grandmother, 'unless to go peeping in on Kate, when I'd told him she was there. He did that – the risk he took!'

He was my father, thought Kate, *and he'd never seen his daughter.*

The things that had worried and mystified Kate suddenly explained themselves as she listened to her grandmother. She had worried about her father's entering the house, even with his own key – how he had done so without crossing the beam of darkness, without being seen by her grandmother. The simple answer was that he *had* been seen. At the sight of such a visitor, risen as from the dead, old Mrs Randall had not screamed out or even exclaimed: that was not her way, and she had remembered Kate at the top of the house. In a whisper she had summoned Fred Tranter into her room to speak with her. Perhaps she had tried to persuade him to go away ... Perhaps she had threatened him, if he stayed ...

But Fred Tranter had done what he had resolved to do, with all the determination of a hesitant man who has made up his mind on a true impulse.

Then he had left the house.

But how? Kate now guessed the answer to that mystery. Instead of going out at once through the front door, her father had slipped into her grandmother's room, as the quickest, safest way for the time being. So, when Kate had questioned her grandmother through the part open doorway, her father had been there, only a breath away from her, behind the very door on whose panelling her hand had rested.

Seeing it all clearly now, understanding it all, Kate stood on the stairs, motionless: she could not have moved even if she had wanted to, she could not stop listening. She listened to her grandmother's voice telling, describing, explaining; and the voice was not interrupted by any other. Mrs Tranter never cried out in amazement, never spoke, never even murmured or sighed. Except for the cold, old voice of Granny Randall and the tiny sound of jam stirring in the pan, there was silence.

Yet Kate knew her mother was there, and must be listening.

Her grandmother had at last reached the subject of the pillow stuffed with money. She had amassed her hoard of banknotes 'against a rainy day', against some day of pressing need, even of disaster. That day came, old Mrs Randall was saying, when Frederick Tranter came home. It was after that day that she had painfully climbed to the loft to recover her hoard. She must have it by her against Frederick Tranter's next visit.

For he would turn up again, old Mrs Randall was saying, like the bad penny he was. A no-good. An outcast, with cowardice and murder behind him ...

Kate listened, a statue on the stairs.

Her grandmother was saying that her money was intended for Frederick Tranter. On his next visit – which would surely come, she said – she would offer him the money. She would pay him handsomely to go away, to stay away, to leave his family in peace, for good. And old Mrs Randall had no doubt that he would take her bribe and go. He was that sort of fellow.

Kate, listening, cried silently to herself: 'It isn't true – it can't be true!' But there was no word of protest from the listener in the kitchen. Old Mrs Randall had stopped talking now; and still there was no sound except for the tiny, soft sound of a long spoon on the stir.

Kate was beaten – she knew it. Whatever she did now – however she rushed and shouted her way into the kitchen – she was only a child. They would not listen to her, pay any attention to her.

Besides, what had she to say except simply that her father could not be like that? He would never take money to do that. She had faith in him – although, indeed, she had no reason with her faith; and her faith by itself could do nothing.

She could do nothing. Nobody could do anything.

Except – except her father himself. He alone could show that these words were all lies.

She must be quick. She began to hurry down the remaining stairs on tiptoe. She meant to make no sound, but a voice called sharply from the kitchen: 'Kate?'

Kate leapt the last few steps to the hall and to her bicycle there. She seized it and pushed it before her out through the door into the garden –

'Kate!' called her mother's voice, trying to halt her.

– and out through the garden door and into the street and away. She had escaped!

She pedalled frantically at first. Then she realized that

she must settle to a pace that would last her to Sattin. This was the third time that she had cycled this way. This time she must not rest or lose her way or dawdle or daydream. She must get to Sattin and her father.

She closed her mind to the thought of how long it would take her to reach Sattin, and then, again, how long it might take her father to get back to Ipston. She would not think of whether he might be too late to put right what had been put so carefully wrong. At least, he was the only person in the whole world who could do what should be done – what *must* be done.

She had not the slightest doubt that her father would be there, in Sattin, waiting for her.

Chapter 20

HOMECOMING

Kate had nearly reached Sattin when she stopped to pump up her tyre for the third time. The slow puncture had become a quick one. The third pumping lasted a very short while indeed: there was really no point in her pumping up again any more.

She got off her crippled bicycle. She wanted to sit down by the side of the road and cry; but that was no good. She must go on, even without a bicycle; and she must hurry.

Then she wanted to fling her bicycle down and begin running. But she must keep her head. Quickly she wheeled her bicycle inside a field gate and left it leaning on the inside of the hedge. She marked the place in her mind by a dead elm that stood there.

Now, on foot, she began the last stretch of road into Sattin. The afternoon was still sunny, hot: she knew she could not run all the way; better to walk steadily and fast.

Coming into Sattin, she saw the shopkeeper putting up his old-fashioned shutters for the weekend. He did not see Kate. He went inside, shut the shop-door and twirled the hanging notice round so that it said CLOSED.

As late as that?

She reached Nanny Tranter's cottage. Her grandmother was in the front garden, tying up tomato plants. She saw who was coming: 'Kate!'

'Nanny, I want my dad.' Something in Kate's voice made her grandmother instantly attentive; no question, no arguing. 'He's not here, Kate. He went down to the shore for a swim.'

'I must get him; but I'm so tired. Would Mr West take me there in his van?'

'Kate, he's gone somewhere.'

'Then I must walk.'

She began at once. Running after her, old Mrs Tranter cried: 'But I'll go for you – I'll go!'

Kate did not even answer. She knew that, tired as she was, she would go more quickly than the little old woman. For a while she heard her grandmother's feet pattering after her, but soon she heard them no more. The old woman had turned back.

Then Kate was alone with the track ahead that she must beat. It was an enemy that she must beat. She must beat it, or be beaten. And she could not be beaten; she could not be defeated.

So on she went, telling herself that her father was waiting for her on Sattin Shore. Yet how late it was – how hopelessly late! She began to run. She ran only a little way, gasping and sobbing; then she had to slow to a walk again.

She longed to stop – to lean against that tree that grew at the curve of the track, or to sit down here on the cool grass at the side of the track – only for a minute. Or to lie flat on her back forever with the earth of the track beneath her and her face upwards to the sky.

But she never stopped. She walked, she trotted, she sometimes even ran again for a little, stumbling and staggering, nearly beaten, yet going on.

The worst came at the end. At the end of the track, the little path that mounted the embankment was almost too much for her. Head hanging down between her shoulders, she went up on all fours, grunting with the effort of her movements.

At the top, she lifted her head to look.

The estuary ...

Sattin Shore, to right, to left. To right, to left, not a soul to be seen. Only the birds of the estuary swimming, flying, pacing along the shore.

She looked, and could not even weep.

Then, almost straight ahead of her – how had she missed it? – she saw a little pile of things that were clothes, and a towel lying on top. Looking next over the estuary waters, she perceived something dark that moved: the head of a swimmer.

Then she pulled herself over the ridge of the bank and ran down the slope of the shore to the edge of the water and right into it. She stood with the ripples washing her dirty, tired legs, and she waved her arms and called aloud – but her voice came from her in a scream: 'Dad!'

She screamed again at the top of her voice; and he heard her, then saw her. The pale blur of his face turned towards her, and he was swimming in. When he was still a long way out in the water, he could already stand, and he began wading ashore in hurried, splashing strides.

He had been swimming naked, as the place was deserted; and so Kate saw her father as Eve saw Adam, newly created, in the Garden of Eden.

But he made at once for his clothes, wrapped the towel round his middle, and came towards her.

'Katy!'

Now, at last, she began to cry.

He took her in his wet arms, kissed her. 'My Kate! Tell me – tell me: what is it?'

So still there must be another effort! She stopped crying, and began the telling. She was too tired to explain properly. She told everything, muddling up the important and the unimportant – strawberry jam and a blue suitcase and the man who had said 'The grave is mine house' and the slow puncture and what Granny Randall had said and what Nanny Tranter had said. But the most important thing, Kate knew, was what Granny Randall had said, and Kate told that, and told it again, and then again.

She felt his hands tightening on her arms as he listened.

She was ending: 'So you must come home quickly: you must come home to say it's not true: you must show that it's not true: you must come home for that.'

'I must. Now.' He was dressing; and, when he was dressed, he took her by the hand and began hurrying her up the shore to the embankment. 'Come on!' he said roughly; and she went with him, although she hardly could.

They topped the embankment – and there was Arnold West's white van. It had just arrived, and turned, ready for the journey back. Arnold West was in the driver's seat, and Nanny Tranter sat beside him. 'Get in!' he said to the two who had just appeared; and they did. He asked where they needed to go – that was his only question. They dropped Nanny Tranter off at her house, and then drove on into Ipston.

Outside old Mrs Randall's house, Arnold West stopped the van: here he would wait. The other two got out, and mounted the steps to the front door. With his free hand – he still held Kate by the other – Fred Tranter found the key that opened the door. They went in.

Together father and daughter entered the house, crossing a line of vision from the left, a beam of darkness.

The kitchen door was open, showing the kitchen empty of people. The jam had been made: Kate saw the jampots ranged along the dresser, the preserving pan back in its place, scoured shiny.

How late it was! – Too late?

The door to the left, the door that always stood ajar, began to creep more widely open.

Fred Tranter let go of Kate's hand to put his own two hands round his mouth and halloo – bellow, rather – up into the house: 'Kitty!' (So that was what her father called her mother, and she had never known!)

The door to the left was opening wide. The movement caught Fred Tranter's eye. He turned his head. He saw old Mrs Randall in the doorway, and he opened his mouth to say something – something terrible perhaps, Kate thought. And then, behind the figure in the doorway, he saw the blue suitcase.

'Aaargh!' he cried, as if he had seen some loathsome, immediately dangerous creature. He darted forward, regardless of the old woman, who staggered against the side of the door, blown there by the gale of his headlong movement.

He seized the case and flung it sideways from him so that it shot out of the bedroom on to the floor of the hall. The case could not have been securely fastened, for it burst open on impact, and two pillows – homely in their covering of old-fashioned black-and-white striped ticking – skidded across the floor.

'Kitty!' he shouted again – and there she was.

Kate had seen her mother running down the stairs from her bedroom; and now she had stopped on the bottom step of the stairs. Her face seemed to Kate to be the face of someone she had never known before. Kate was afraid.

Kitty Tranter looked at her husband, her face lit

white with anger that had burnt in her for a long, long time. 'Ten years!' she said. 'Ten years!' Then: 'Why have you come now? Is it the money? Is that really true?'

He was already grabbing at the nearer pillow, tearing at it. 'For *that*?' he shouted. 'You think I came back for *that*?' The ticking, half rotten with age, gave under such violent handling, and from the sudden rent spurted a snowstorm.

It was the wrong pillow!

A storm of little feathers enveloped the angry man, bemusing him in an instant. Round him they swirled, brown-shaded, cream-speckled, or white as snowflakes; and the tiniest fluffs wavered, dipped and were already settling on any convenient projection of Fred Tranter. One settled on an eyebrow, to dangle from it like a rock-climber; another, tiny but dauntless, adventured to a nostril and, on an inhalation, abruptly disappeared from view. Then Fred Tranter's nose wrinkled in a kind of horror, his eyelids clenched shut, his whole body stiffened. Inside him, like rolling thunder, the sneeze menaced and struggled and at last burst out in the loudest, longest *Atishoo!* that Kate had ever heard – and the fluff shot from his nostril again like a rabbit from a rabbit-hole, on such a blast of air that all the downy feathers that had begun to drift drowsily to rest were suddenly blown up round him again in a great swirl and swarm of alarm.

As Kitty Tranter witnessed this happening, her face changed. Kate could not at first tell what the change was, except that something icy seemed to melt, something stony seemed to crumble. Then Kate saw her mother's eyes half close, her head tipped back, her mouth widened and opened, and she was gasping, with almost a hooting sound: 'Oh! Oh! Oh!'

'You're laughing – *laughing*!' In rage Fred Tranter snatched up the remaining pillow. One end seemed a little open, and he forced his hand in – right in – and tore the pillow inside out. Out flew more downy feathers; but not many. The rest of the filling was banknotes. He plucked out and scattered the notes in a frenzy to be rid of them: they fell more heavily than the feathers had done, eddied only briefly, then settled in drifts round his feet and round Kate's and round the feet of the old woman who still stood, disregarded, in her doorway. She was the only one who, at last, stooped low and began to gather them up.

'Kitty, you don't still believe that I've come for the money, do you – do you?'

Kitty Tranter had stopped laughing. She put out a hand towards Fred Tranter. He went, trampling the paper money underfoot, to take it.

'Let's talk, Kitty.' His voice asked, implored.

'Yes,' said Kitty Tranter. 'Alone.' She answered her husband, but she looked at her mother. The old woman ceased her money-gathering to look up; their gazes met. Kitty Tranter looked steadily, with a resolution that was much more than defiance; old Mrs Randall dropped her gaze, turned and went back into her room, shutting the door behind her.

'I hate this house,' said Fred Tranter. 'Where can we go?'

'Out.'

'Oh!' cried Kate softly, in dismay; and her mother was instantly aware of her there, as she had hardly been before.

'We can't leave Kate here now,' said Mrs Tranter. 'And the other two won't be back for hours perhaps.'

'Arnie West's outside with his van,' said Kate's father. 'He'll look after her for a bit.'

Kate did not want to be left with Arnold West; but it would be of no use to say that.

Her father opened the front door again and called into the street: 'Arnold, we need your help!'

Chapter 21

IN THE CAFÉ

Arnold West had not stirred in his seat since he had stopped the van. Syrup, approaching along the front of the terrace, judged that the van was not only parked but driverless, or as good as driverless. He leapt up on to the bonnet and eyed the dark shape on the other side of the windscreen. A man; but he never moved. Syrup collapsed gracefully on his back on the bonnet of the van, stretched his paws forward on either side of his paunch, and, craning, began to clean his belly-fur with his tongue.

Arnold West never moved. He sat there in his van while indoors the feathers and the banknotes flew and Fred and Kitty Tranter spoke to each other again after a silence of more than ten bitter years.

He was thinking intently; and he was remembering.

Syrup finished his cleaning. He looked towards the house: the front door was beginning to open. But something had made Syrup decide that – just now – the house was not the place for him. He slipped down from the bonnet of the van and sauntered away.

The front door opened, and Kate was coming out towards the van.

'Arnold, we need your help!' From behind Kate came her father's voice, confiding her for the time being to the care of Arnold West. Fred Tranter suggested that Arnie took Kate to have tea somewhere. He had given her money for that.

Neither of them was pleased. Kate climbed into the front of the van beside the driver, but kept as far from him as possible. Arnold turned a cheerless face towards her: 'I don't know that we can get tea as late as this in Ipston. Places are mostly shutting by now. I don't know anywhere.'

'I don't want tea,' said Kate. (But oh! she did! And whatever would they do with their time together, if they did not have tea?)

'We'd better go somewhere,' said Arnold West. He started the engine, but let it run.

Then Kate remembered her bicycle. She explained eagerly that she had had to leave it hidden behind a hedge, to be collected later. She would recognize the place by the gateway and the dead elm.

The straightforwardness of this task pleased them both. They took the van back towards Sattin, and picked up the bicycle. It went easily into the rear of the van.

'I've been thinking,' said Arnold West. 'There's a place on the main road that might still be open and do us a meal.'

It was open – just. The last customers were leaving, and a boy was already sweeping the floor, having piled the chairs upside-down on the tables. He was persuaded to take two chairs down and set them at a table and to lay cutlery and cruets. Then he went off to the kitchen with an order for eggs and chips and a pot of tea.

They sat at their table in silence, waiting. The café was now deserted; the boy with the broom did not return. The interior of the café seemed very dim, although there was still plenty of daylight outside. Showing strongly black against the lightness from the windows, scores of legs of upside-down chairs surrounded them at head height.

After a while, Arnold West said: 'I go down to Sattin Shore a good deal; I have done for years. There are shore birds I watch.'

'Oh yes?' said Kate. The conversation promised to be dull, but safe.

'Shelduck ... mallard ... widgeon ... And I've seen cormorants. Have you ever seen cormorants?'

'No,' said Kate.

'Strange birds. I've seen some strange things on Sattin Shore.'

Kate said nothing; she knew nothing about birds.

'Curlews,' said Arnold West. 'Have you ever heard curlews at night? They call as they fly in the dark. Have you heard them?'

'No,' said Kate.

'They sound like children crying – I've often thought that. Like lost children crying.'

'That's strange,' said Kate.

After a while, Arnold West said, 'You never knew your Uncle Bob ...'

'No.'

'You wouldn't have forgotten him, if you'd known him.'

'No?'

'He was good-looking. Brains, too. But more than that: he made you want to be with him; where he was, that was the best place to be. He was always like that, even at school.'

'Were you at school with him, then?'

'Yes, in Ipston.'

'And with my dad?'

'Yes,' said Arnold West, but with indifference.

'What was he like – my dad, I mean?'

'All right, I suppose. But not like Bob. He hadn't the ways Bob had. Nobody else had Bob's ways ...'

Kate said firmly: 'I like my dad.'

After a pause, Arnold West began again: 'Strange things I've seen on Sattin Shore. You wouldn't know a godwit?'

'A bird?' said Kate. 'No.'

'I've seen hundreds – *hundreds* – of black-tailed godwits on Sattin Shore, in the winter.'

'And in the summer?' asked Kate.

'I've seen other things in summer,' said Arnold West. He leaned forward over the table and began to tell her how he would go bird-watching on Sattin Shore, in summer, on moonlit nights.

The café interior was darkening. Kate thought: Surely we shall have a light on soon. We shall have to have a light to eat by and drink by. Besides, I don't like the chairlegs round us, all round us, so close, so dark ...

'I can't ever forget Bob,' said Arnold West. 'I can't forget his dying.' He turned his mild face, blurred white in the dimness, towards Kate; he stared at her. 'And you know the churchyard near your Granny Randall's house?'

'Yes, I do.'

'He was buried there. I was at his funeral. I stood beside your Nan. I was all she had left: one son dead; the other run away. I was all she had. She needed me; she leant on me. She always has done.'

The tea would be coming soon, Kate thought. Then the light – oh, the light!

Arnold West began to speak in low, hurried tones, of an expedition he had made to Sattin Shore one moonlit summer night, many years before. At the beginning of the story there were shore-birds and a man with binoculars, himself.

At the end of the story there were two more men: one was a dead man, who lay drowned on the shore; the other was a man who was running back along the field-track towards the village to get help – help – help –

The light had left the café, the dark was coming in. Kate shut her eyes against darkness and Arnold West's mild, pale face turned towards her and the chairlegs that blackly fenced them in, the two of them, alone together. But Arnold West's voice went on and on, and she had to hear it.

She forced her eyes open again; and everything was still there, the same. The chairlegs and the face and the voice and what the voice had said.

The voice stopped.

Then Kate whispered: 'You were there that night, all the time. You weren't in Sattin Wood with your owls, as you said: you were on Sattin Shore. You saw my dad bring him out of the water. You saw my dad bring him round, and then go off for help. And then . . .'

'I've just told you. I pulled him down below the tide-line. I had to be finished with him.'

Kate stared and stared at him, frightened – and yet he was not a frightening man, really. 'Why?' she said, at last.

'You're only a child. You wouldn't understand.'

'But now you must tell me. You must.'

'He was a friend, and then he betrayed me. He was the only friend I ever had; but he threw me over, and he laughed when I cried. Then – much later – he seemed a friend again. He said he would go into partnership with me: I believed him, and I was happy; but he never meant it. He told me so, later, and he laughed at me for believing it. If he had been a rat, I would have set my dog to kill him.'

'You did kill him.'

Arnold West did not answer.

'You've told me,' said Kate, 'and I shall tell. I must tell.'

'No,' said Arnold West. 'You won't. You can't. They wouldn't believe you. You're a child that makes things up, they say: mysteries; fairy-tales; horrors ... They'll say you made this up; and I shall laugh and say so too.'

'Then why have you told me?'

'I've waited ten years to tell someone. Just one person would be enough. You turned up. You were the right one. I feel better now. *Lighter.*'

'I won't – I won't keep your secret!' cried Kate. 'I'll tell!'

At the back of the café a door opened, and clatter and cooking-smells rushed towards them. The boy's voice called to them, 'Coming now!'

'I'll tell!' Kate cried again.

A click, and the boy had switched on the electric light. The room was filled with light.

Arnold West blinked and blinked. 'Tell what?'

The boy was coming towards them with a loaded tray.

'What you told me.'

'I told you nothing.'

The boy had reached them and was unloading the tray on to the table before them. Kate whispered past him, to Arnold West: 'You mean, you deny it now?'

'Deny *what*?'

Their eggs and chips and pot of tea were before them, so they ate and drank – Arnold West heartily; Kate very little. They did not speak. At the end of the meal, Kate made a last attempt: 'I shall tell my Nan what you told me.'

She thought she had found the weakness in his defence, for he flinched at her words. He cared so much what

Nanny Tranter thought of him. But almost immediately he was secure again in his stronghold.

'Tell her *what*?'

After that, Kate gave up trying.

They drove back into Ipston in silence – they would never have anything more to say to each other, ever. They drove up to the house. The windows of the house blazed with light; everyone was at home.

Arnold West stayed with the van, unloading the bicycle from it. Kate went up to the front door and opened it. They were in the hall, as if they had been waiting there for her all the time.

She stood on the threshold of the house, looking at them.

She saw Randall, and his face was triumphant: what he had been scheming and contriving to happen had at last happened. Lenny's face, as yet, was bewildered and white – the face of someone after a great shock. He was still stunned by the almost unbelievable; later, he would feel. And there was her mother, Kitty Tranter, with her changed face, too: not happier or sadder, not more loving – or more hating. None of those things, or other things that Kate might have expected. Just changed utterly in expression, changed into something new and strange.

And there was her father looking at her: she still knew him so little that she could not tell whether he, too, had altered. It seemed only now that she had time to look at him long and carefully and think: So this is my father. I am partly like him; I am partly him.

She stared at her father – it could have been only for a moment – and he smiled back at her, awkwardly.

Then Kitty Tranter came forward to her daughter: 'We've been waiting for you. We've all of us been waiting . . .'

No, not all. There was no Granny. She had shut herself in her room, with her useless money, and the door that had always stood ajar was now closed.

Chapter 22

ALONG SATTIN SHORE

The return of Fred Tranter from the dead caused less stir – outside his own family – than might have been expected.

In the village of Sattin, more than ten years had softly rubbed away at people's memories. Besides – as old Mrs Tranter pointed out – there were fewer people left in Sattin nowadays to remember the history of the two brothers.

And in Ipston, Fred Tranter had hardly been known at all since his youth. To the astonished Anna, Kate had said, in explanation, only: 'We thought he was dead; and he wasn't.' Brian asked questions, but they were not all answered.

Within the Tranter family, the return made a difference – Kate perceived its hugeness like the uprearing of a mountain peak through clearing mist. Years yet to come would show the extent of the difference made to them all, to Fred Tranter included.

Old Mrs Randall, in her silent way, denied the difference; she shut her door against the fact of it. Fred Tranter, to her, was still what she had always thought him – the bad penny that turned up, a better-dead-than-back-again. She did not try to prevent his entering her house to be with his wife and children; but she shut her private door against him. She would speak only to her daughter and to her daughter's children.

On his side, Fred Tranter remembered – and knew that others must remember, too – the folly of his panic running away all those years ago. But at that time the air had been dark with suspicion, jealousy and black clouds of bitterness. From all this old Mrs Randall had chosen to profit. She had claimed her daughter and her daughter's children for herself; nor had Kitty Tranter been able to resist her mother.

All this was in the past – something that Kate only dimly perceived. She would rather not have perceived it at all, since it made her see, in her mind's eye, Sattin Shore on a moonlit night, and a dead man lying there ...

Kate preferred to look to the future – to her birthday in July, and, beyond that, to the great, good changes that were promised.

'We're thinking of going to Australia,' she said to Anna. 'To settle. All of us. My dad's lived in Australia for years: he's got friends there, and a job waiting for him. So now he wants us to go back to Australia with him.'

This was so very much more than the Johnsons' move away from Ipston that Anna was struck into silence. She recovered to say reproachfully: 'Then we shall never meet again!'

'I'll come back when I'm older, you'll see. Ran says he's only going to have a look at what it's like – Australia, I mean. He might come straight back, he says. If he feels like it.'

'What about his girl friend?'

'Vicky's going to university, so he wouldn't have seen much of her, anyway.'

'What about Lenny and his friends?'

'Lenny's sorry about Brian, but he's glad about everything else. He's never been in an aeroplane, or seen a kangaroo.'

'What about Syrup?'

'He can go with us.'

'But will he *want* to go?'

'You're taking your cat with you, when you move.'

'Not to Australia.'

'Well, Syrup will have to lump Australia, won't he?' said Kate sharply.

'And what about your granny?'

Kate glanced aside from Anna. 'She can go with us, too. My dad says our granny can have a nice little bungalow or a flat or something, all of her own, but near us, in Australia.' (This was what Fred Tranter had brought himself to promise. He intended to honour that promise; but it was hard to him.)

Anna said: 'And your granny wants to go to Australia?'

'No,' said Kate.

Unlike Syrup, Mrs Randall could not be made to lump Australia. She refused to consider leaving Ipston or the house she lived in. If her daughter's family absolutely must go to Australia, then they must; not she. Catharine could talk herself blue in the face, it would make no difference to her.

Nowadays Kitty Tranter was often closeted with her mother; she came away from such talks blankly, or almost in tears.

Kate watched her mother anxiously. 'Shall we all have to stay in Ipston, because of Granny?'

'No!' said her mother. She took Kate into her arms. 'You love me, Kate?'

'Yes.' Of course ... of course ...

'When I was your age, I loved my mother, too; and now I'm the age I am, and she's an old woman, I still love her, but differently, of course. I can't stop loving her

now, *even after everything that's happened*. I can't stop, even
if I wanted to. And I care what becomes of her ... I can't
just desert her ...'

'But how can we get to Australia, then?' Kate loosed
herself angrily from her mother's arms. 'How?'

Her mother did not answer.

At about this time, Kate and Lenny went to stay with
old Mrs Tranter at Sattin, absenting themselves from their
schools by arrangement. Their mother said that this
would be a summer holiday for them, and leave her more
free to do the things that needed doing at home. More
free, Kate thought shrewdly, to try to talk their granny
round to Australia.

Their father drove them to Sattin in the second-hand
car he had now bought for such purposes. Their mother
came too, and Syrup in his cat-basket. This was the first
time that young Mrs Tranter and old Mrs Tranter had
met since the birth of Kate. They were very polite, but
with little to say to each other, and Kate could see that
Nanny Tranter was flustered. The old woman was plainly
much relieved when the car drove off, leaving her with
her two grandchildren.

There were no other children to play with in Sattin;
but Kate, at least, was content to be with her new
grandmother, and with Syrup. He took to country life
immediately, seeming not to miss the town pleasures of
brick walls and dustbins. He would often stay out all night,
coming back at breakfast time with leaves from Sattin
Wood caught in his fur and with a ravenous appetite.
Whenever he could, in the daytime, he slept in old Mrs
Tranter's lap as she sat – Kate had rarely been so favoured.

'I shall miss him, if you all go to Australia,' said the
old woman, and sighed. She spoilt Syrup, and he liked
it.

Meanwhile, Lenny was bored, until he discovered

Arnold West's fruitfarm next door. He was soon spending most of his time there. Old Mrs Tranter nodded placidly over his preoccupation, but Kate was uneasy. 'Why do you go there so often, Lenny?'

'He lets me drive his tractor. And you should see the tools he has! He lets me use them.'

'I don't like him,' said Kate.

Lenny considered. 'I don't *like* him, but I can do interesting things there. And he's harmless.'

'He never tells you anything?'

'What should he tell?'

Kate left it at that.

Kate's birthday came while they were still in Sattin. It seemed less important than it had done in other years, because other important things were happening, or likely to happen. Kate realized that some people would have thought the other things much more important.

On the birthday morning, Lenny gave Kate his usual present of sweets, and old Mrs Tranter gave her a book of animal pictures that had once, she said, belonged to 'the boys'. Inside the book she wrote Kate's name and Kate's age on that birthday, and her own name 'with love and kisses' – all very crabbedly in violet ink.

Later, Fred Tranter came to fetch them to a birthday tea in Ipston. 'Won't you come too, Nan?' Kate had asked. Old Mrs Tranter shook her head fearfully: 'I don't go so far from home nowadays. I'll be waiting here for you, when you come back.'

What a timid little creature she was! Kate thought. She would no more venture to Ipston than she would emigrate to Australia. (That had once been suggested to her, but only once: she had been so frightened by the idea.)

Kate's birthday tea in old Mrs Randall's house was a family affair. The only one missing was Mrs Randall herself: she stayed shut in her room and would not join the party. Kate had to take a slice of birthday cake in to her.

Mrs Randall looked at the cake with its pink-and-white icing and the tiny, half-burnt-down pink candle: 'You've had no present from me yet, on this birthday of yours.'

'It doesn't matter, Granny. Honestly.'

'I'll give you something of my own to remember me by. To remember me by when you're far away and I'm left here. To remember me by when I'm dead and gone one day.'

Kate wished angrily that she didn't feel like crying.

'Which of my things do you fancy, then?'

'I don't want anything ...'

'Not even my big black tray?'

'Oh, Granny!' The snow – the snow! And the speed going down Gripe's Hill on the big black tray! And the party afterwards – sitting next to Ran and drinking tea out of a big yellow mug! 'Oh, Granny, thank you!'

'Take it.' The old woman had the tray already leaning at the back of her chair, so all the time this was what she had intended giving. Kate received it and held it against herself, like a breastplate against affliction. 'And take care of it. Don't bang it. Don't batter it. *Don't toboggan on it.*' Startlingly, old Mrs Randall cackled with laughter. 'But you'll have to manage without snow in Australia, won't you? For you're going, you know; and I'm staying.'

Kate did not know what to say to that; but old Mrs Randall expected no answer. She began eating her slice of birthday cake.

Kate went back to the kitchen. She showed the others her gift, and told them what her grandmother had said – except about the tobogganing.

Mrs Tranter said: 'Yes, it's all settled about Australia.

We really are going, and your granny has chosen to stay here, and it will all be all right for her. Granny's going to let the house to lodgers, and the lodgers will help her and look after her. The vicar is sure he can find the right kind of lodgers for her.'

So that was all right, at last!

Later that afternoon, Kate's birthday treat – chosen by herself – was a visit to Sattin Shore. She wanted only her mother and father to go with her. Kitty Tranter, turning her head aside, had said quietly: 'I'd rather not go'; but Fred Tranter, equally low voiced, had said: 'You must, Kitty.'

Kate had pretended not to hear.

When they got to Sattin Shore, the tide was out; the shore was spacious. They strolled along it, Kate in the middle. At first, she was abreast of the other two, then she began to lag behind.

She lagged further and further behind, until she was walking alone along the shore, with the others distantly ahead. She was glad to have them there, and yet to be on her own. She wandered irregularly between the far-out rippling edge of the water and the thin, bright green fringe of weed, combed all one way by the fingers of the tide, that marked its last highest reach.

Seaweed lay on the shore. Seagulls floated and wheeled in the air high above. The smell of the sea was on the air that Kate breathed. Of the sea itself, there was neither sight nor sound; but Kate knew that its waters crept up the estuary as far as Sattin Shore, and further. The up-flowing tide of the sea met the down-flowing of the river; their meeting was without conflict or turmoil. The waters met, mingled . . .

'Kate!' Her mother's voice called her distantly but sharply. Kate ran to catch up.

Her father was saying: 'Must you, Kitty?'

'I must ... Listen, Kate. You know that your Uncle Bob was drowned on this shore?'

'Yes, I know.'

'There were rumours afterwards, false, cruel rumours that you may hear of one day – if you have not already heard of them. You're old enough to be told this, Kate; and I tell you now to forewarn you: always remember that whatever happened that night – however your uncle came to die – your father had no hand in his dying.'

Kate could not help testing them, by saying, 'Then whose fault was it?'

Her father said: 'Nobody's.'

Nobody ... In her mind, this sunny shore darkened and darkened, and under cover of the dark a man crept down to the shore ... She shivered. Aloud she said: 'I wish – oh, I wish that I hadn't been born just then, in the middle of that very night, when Uncle Bob died. In the dark, when he died, just after midnight.'

Her mother, surprised, laughed. 'You born that very night? What nonsense! You were born hours and hours later, in the afternoon of that day. I was very ill, but I remember seeing the afternoon sun on your bald head when they showed you to me first. You were born at about teatime.'

Suddenly the shore was sunny again, and Kate was happy. She had been born at teatime – when fresh tea is made in the pot, and bread and butter is spread with strawberry jam, and birthday cakes have their candles lit.

'Let's go back now,' said Kate; and all three turned and walked back, not quite by the way they had come, but along the top of the estuary bank, beside the cornfields. The larks were still singing high above the cornfields; and Fred Tranter promised to take his daughter swimming off the shore one day soon, when the tide was coming in. That was the safe time.

They took her back to Nanny Tranter's, where Lenny already was, and left her there.

That night, at bedtime, Kate told her grandmother the news that Australia was a settled thing.

The old woman said, 'I'm glad for you all.'

'But you'll miss us – you'll mind?'

There was a long silence. Then: 'There are things we must bear.' Kate took her grandmother's hand in her own and held it, and felt the thin fingers grip hers as though they would never let go. Then old Mrs Tranter relaxed her grip: she took her hand gently from Kate's and left Kate's lying there, free.

Kate asked: 'You'll go on living here, all alone?' For an instant she thought of her other granny's lodgers; but she could not see Nanny Tranter managing a cottageful of lodgers – and who would want to lodge in Sattin, anyway?

'Some day soon, Kate, I shall go and live with Arnie West. For a long time now he's wanted me to do that, so that he can look after me better.'

Kate said, as she had said to Lenny: 'I don't like Arnold West.'

Her grandmother said: 'I've known Arnie since he was a child younger than you are now. His parents were no-goods, so he turned to me. He turned to me to love him, I mean. So I did. I've gone on loving him. You can't just stop, for a reason.'

'I don't like him,' Kate said obstinately.

Her grandmother sighed.

Later that night, Kate was in bed when the door opened softly and her grandmother stole in. She was in her night-dress, and she carried something in her arms.

'Still awake, Kate?'

'Yes . . .'

'I've brought you Syrup. He'd settled for the night on

my bed, but I thought you'd like him.' A soft descent of heaviness at Kate's feet.

Kate said: 'I've been awake, thinking.'

'Yes?' Old Mrs Tranter was sitting on the bed beside Syrup, stroking him, coaxing him to stay there. Kate, from her pillow, could just make our her grandmother's face, small with age, and yet childish-looking with the white hair in two night-time plaits on either side of the face. Such an innocent, defenceless little old woman, Kate thought ...

'Nanny, I wish you wouldn't go and live with Arnold West. Perhaps, if you knew what he was really like – if you really knew ...'

Kate thought the old woman had not heard her, for she did not answer at once. Then she said: 'You think I don't know Arnie. It's true I haven't always understood – I'm not quick-witted, like your other granny. That terrible time when Bob was drowned and Fred ran away and I was left with Arnie – oh, I didn't understand then!' She bowed her head over Syrup, so that Kate could not see her face. 'But, in all the time since then, I've come to know Arnie. What I haven't known, I've guessed. I know now some of the things in poor Arnie's mind. I know the thing *on* his mind ...'

The old woman lifted her face again; but, peering, Kate could not read its expression. What had her grandmother meant, exactly?

In a voice so low that Kate could hardly catch the words, Mrs Tranter said: 'On his conscience ...'

Kate was appalled: 'You know ...'

In the same low voice, Mrs Tranter said: 'It's very hard to know some things; but we must bear knowledge. And that's not all. Arnie thinks because I'm small and old and weak that I need him; but really poor Arnie needs me. He needs someone to love him, and I couldn't fail him in that.' The old woman began to get up from the bed. In the dimness her shape was small, insignificant; but Kate thought suddenly, She's like a rock – that's what people mean when they say 'firm as a rock, steadfast as a rock'. Size and all the rest have nothing to do with it. She's a rock.

The old woman had turned to go back to her bedroom.

'Wait!' said Kate. 'Don't go!'

'Kate, I don't want to talk like this any more,' said Mrs Tranter piteously.

'But it's about something else,' said Kate. 'It's about Syrup. I've been thinking how he'll hate – *hate* – that long journey to Australia; and he may hate Australia, too. He loves living with you. He'd be much, much happier staying here, keeping you company.'

Agitated, old Mrs Tranter took a step back towards the bed. 'Oh, my dear! Think – think how you'd miss him!'

'But you'd like to have him, for company?'

'I'd love to have him. But think, my dear –'

'I'll think,' promised Kate. But, in her mind, painfully, she had already thought, and decided; and she was glad.

Her grandmother came back again to kiss her good night. 'Don't think of it now. Go to sleep now, and sleep well.' The old woman left her, closing the door as she went.

Kate began to fall asleep. She felt the soft lightening of weight as Syrup moved off the bed to some more reliably comfortable position elsewhere. He left her, but Kate did not mind.

Deeply, dreamlessly, she slept.